Elle Woods

Blonde Love

Elle Woods

Blonde Love

Based on the character
created by Amanda Brown

Story by Natalie Standiford

HYPERION PAPERBACKS FOR CHILDREN
New York

First Edition

1 3 5 7 9 10 8 6 4 2

Library of Congress Cataloging-in-Publication Data on file
ISBN 0-7868-3888-4

Visit www.hyperionteens.com

Elle Woods

Blonde Love

Chapter 1

Roses are red, magenta, maroon;
Valentine's Day is coming soon. Give
your love a lacy heart, and chocolates if
you're really smart; a fancy dinner à la
carte. Go, Bees!

"I DON'T SEE what that cheer has to do with basket-ball," Chessie Morton said, dropping her pom-pom on the floor.

"It doesn't," P. J. Stoller said.

"Yes, it does," Elle Woods said. "Love is part of everything. Even basketball."

"Oh, no," Chessie said. "Elle's been taken over by the Blonde Buddha again."

1

"It's not Buddhism," Elle said. "It's valentine fever! Let's try it one more time."

Elle led the cheerleading squad through the cheer once more. Most of the girls had the moves down already, but Chessie missed a step and kicked Chloe Gaitskill by mistake. Chloe gave her a dirty look.

"Okay, I guess we can quit for today," Elle said. "But let's practice extra hard tomorrow. We've got to get the new cheers down before the game on Friday."

Elle Woods, as the captain of the Beverly Hills High School cheerleading squad, was responsible for writing most of the cheers. Whatever was on her mind tended to come out in the rhymes. And love was on her mind.

Valentine's Day was only a few weeks away. And she had special plans.

The cheerleaders broke formation and went to the locker room. "Chloe, I love your new haircut," Chessie said.

Chloe's long, straight blonde hair had once hung halfway down her back. Now it was chopped into chic shoulder-length blonde chunks.

"Is that a Val?" Chessie asked.

"What's a Val?" Elle asked.

"You don't know what a Val is?" Chessie said. "Sometimes you're so out of it it's cute, Elle. You know, the Val. It's the hot new haircut, invented by Valerie Vernay, stylist to the stars."

"Oh, right," Elle said. It all sounded vaguely familiar to her. "I think I saw that on *Access Hollywood*."

"My mother got me an appointment with Valerie Vernay herself," Chloe said. "Which is practically impossible. But Mom is friends with the head of Bluestone Pictures, so, you know . . ." Everybody knew. Her mom had pulled some strings. "I saw Tippi Hanover at the salon."

"You look just like Tippi now," Chessie said. "Only prettier."

Tippi Hanover was a rising-star teen actress. Everyone wanted to look like her. She was one of the stars who had made Valerie Vernay famous.

"Thanks," said Chloe, happily taking the compliment. "I think I'll go to Pacifico tonight and show it off." Pacifico was a trendy dance club, very popular with Beverly Hills students.

"You're going to Pacifico?" Chessie said. "What a coincidence! I was going to go to Pacifico tonight, too. Let's go together."

Chloe shrugged. "Sure, whatever. Do you want

to come along with us, Elle?"

"I'd love to, but I'm busy," Elle said.

"Oh?" Chessie said. "Seeing Hunter tonight?"

Hunter Perry was Elle's boyfriend. He was a freshman at UCLA.

"I wish," Elle said. "He's got basketball practice, and then some kind of frat meeting. I've got to get ready for the student senate meeting tomorrow." In addition to being the captain of the cheerleaders, Elle was also student body president.

"You and Hunter are both so busy, I don't know how you ever see each other," Chloe said.

"It's hard," Elle said. "But we made a promise to see each other at least once a week, no matter what."

"You're smart to schedule your dates," Chessie said. "That way Hunter can't get out of them."

"I don't think he wants to get out of them," Elle said. "He told me he wishes he could see me more often."

"He was always such a flatterer," Chessie said. "Silver Tongue. That's what Savannah used to call him."

Savannah Shaw was the former cheerleading captain of Beverly Hills High—and Hunter's ex-girlfriend. She was the kind of girl every other girl wished she could be. But she'd graduated the year before. Even though she was gone, Chessie still liked to bring up her name once in a while. Elle didn't mind. It helped keep her on her toes.

Elle took off her cheer shorts and changed into designer jeans and a plaid blazer. "Wait till Hunter sees what I have planned for Valentine's Day."

She'd spent hours imagining that romantic evening. "We're going to have dinner at my house, out by the pool. Bernard will help me cook, and Zosia promised to help set up the table, with flowers and candles and everything, so it'll be super-romantic."

Elle's parents lived in a beautiful modern house in Brentwood. It had a pool, of course, and servants' quarters. Bernard was their butler and Zosia their maid—but by now the two were more like family.

Elle imagined herself sitting with Hunter in the moonlight on a warm southern California evening, just the two of them, trading chocolate-covered strawberries and kisses . . .

"That sounds so nice," P.J. said. "I wish Craig would do romantic things like that." She'd been going out with Craig Jenkins, but it wasn't serious. "I'll probably spend Valentine's Day at home watching *American Idol*."

"Matt's taking me to the Lakers game," Tamila Vines complained. Her boyfriend, Matt Reiss, was a basketball fanatic, but he was too short to make the Beverly Hills High team. So he had become manager instead. "He bought the tickets before he realized it was Valentine's Day."

"Everybody knows Valentine's Day is February fourteenth," P.J. said. "Spacing on that is so *boy*."

"Well, I'm going to do something fabulous on Valentine's Day," Chessie said.

"Really?" Elle said. "What?"

"I don't know yet," Chessie said. "But it's going to rock."

"Everybody should celebrate Valentine's Day, whether they're in love or not," Elle said. "I think there should be parties everywhere, all over the city, for everyone."

"Why don't we have a big party here at school?" Tamila said.

"That's a great idea," Elle said. "Maybe we will." As president, she had the power to get things like that done.

Chessie tightened the belt on her safari jacket. "Oh, Elle, I almost forgot to tell you. Guess who's friends with Hunter? My next-door neighbor, Julia Gables."

"Really?" Elle said. "That's a funny coincidence."

"I *know*," Chessie said. "She's a freshman at UCLA, too, and they have *two* classes together, Sociology and Psych. Of course, as soon as I realized she was going to UCLA, I asked if she knew Hunter. Turns out they're good friends."

"Is she nice?" Elle asked.

"*So* nice," Chessie said. "And gorgeous. She's tall, with long dark hair and green eyes like a cat's. She kind of reminds me of Savannah, only not blonde."

Elle felt a twinge of jealousy, but it faded quickly. She had used to think that Savannah was Hunter's ideal girl. Hunter was tall, and so was Savannah. Elle was an adorable blonde with great taste in clothes, but she was on the petite side. But she and Hunter had been together for eight months now. She wasn't worried about tall girls anymore. She was over that now. Totally secure.

"I'm glad Hunter's making friends," Elle said. "Not that it's hard for him."

"Has he mentioned Julia to you?" Chessie asked.

"No," Elle said.

"That's funny," Chessie said. "Julia made it sound like she sees him all the time."

"He can't mention every person he meets at

school, Chessie," P.J. said.

"I know," Chessie said. "I'm just saying . . ."

"I'm not worried," Elle said. "I know Hunter loves me. And I trust him. One hundred percent."

"When's your next date?" Chessie asked.

"Saturday night," Elle said. "Three whole days away." It seemed like forever. Elle wished she could see Hunter every day.

"A lot can happen in three whole days," Chessie said.

"Yeah," Chloe said. "In three days you could get laryngitis and stop talking, Chessie."

"Chessie could never stop talking," P.J. said. "Even if she had her tongue surgically removed."

"I heard about this girl in Malibu who did that to make her cheekbones more prominent," Tamila said.

"What? No way," Chloe said. "That wasn't her tongue. It was her back teeth."

"Can you talk without your back teeth?" P.J. said.

"Of course," Chloe said. "But you can't eat as much, so it helps keep you thin, which makes your cheekbones stick out even more."

"Chessie could talk without her tongue, her teeth, or her lips," P.J. said. "If you sewed her mouth shut, she'd figure out a way to talk through her nose."

"Hey," Chessie said, looking hurt, "I'm not some kind of talking freak."

Elle felt sorry for her. "Don't pick on Chessie," she said. "She's only trying to give me a Hunter news flash. To be nice."

"Sure she is," Chloe said.

Chapter 2

"THAT'S SO TYPICAL of Chessie," Laurette said, "to live next door to some girl who goes to school with Hunter. Can it really be a coincidence? I wouldn't be surprised if she planted Julia at UCLA just to mess things up between you."

Laurette Smythe was Elle's best friend. She was a determined noncheerleader with brown hair and a taste for vintage clothes. That day, as she and Elle strolled down Melrose Avenue, she was wearing a sixties psychedelic-print minidress with white go-go boots. Elle wore a Marc Jacobs sundress.

It was Saturday, and Elle was shopping for something new to wear on her date with Hunter that night. Her teacup Chihuahua, Underdog, trotted ahead of her on his metallic gold leash.

"You're so paranoid," Elle said. "First of all, nothing is messed up between us. Second of all, of course Chessie wouldn't plant someone at UCLA. How could she?"

"You're right," Laurette said. "She'd want to be there herself. It would be more like her to pose as a student."

"Poor Chessie," Elle said. "Why is everybody always so suspicious of her?"

"Because she's always up to something," Laurette said. She stopped in front of a plate-glass store window. "Now *that*—that is *you.*"

"You think?" Elle looked at the dress on the mannequin. It was a red cashmere shift with a big pink heart over the chest. Elle loved pink and hearts. But she was beginning to wonder if that weren't a little too girlish. Maybe she should start dressing in a more sophisticated style, now that her boyfriend was in college.

"Totally," Laurette said. "It screams, 'Elle! Buy me, Elle!'"

Elle picked Underdog up. "What do you think?" she asked him. He barked twice, which she took to mean "Try it on."

"You're right," Elle said. "It would be perfect for

Valentine's Day." She could never resist anything with a heart on it.

They went inside the store. Elle tried on the dress. It fit perfectly. "I'll wear it tonight," she said. "As a sort of Valentine's Day preview."

Hunter picked her up at seven in his Mercedes convertible. Elle's heart raced as soon as she heard the doorbell. She peeked out the window and saw him standing at the front door in his blue-striped button-down shirt and jeans. He caught her peeking and waved.

Elle's mother, Eva Woods, answered the door. She loved Hunter. Elle could hear her gushing over him from all the way down the hall. A few minutes later Eva tapped on her door.

"Guess who's *heee*re, Elle," she said, her voice rising. She often got giddy around Hunter.

"I'll be right *theee*re," Elle said. She checked her new dress once more in the mirror. Whoops—her ponytail had come loose. She fixed it and tied it with a ribbon. Perfect.

"Here's the pink pussycat," Elle's father, Wyatt, said when she appeared in the living room. Hunter stood up and kissed her on the cheek.

"You look very cute," he said. "New dress?"

"Uh-huh," she said, twirling around.

"Don't keep her out too late," Wyatt said. "Just kidding. You guys have a good time."

"Have fun, you two!" Eva said.

It was a warm, lovely night, so they rode to the beach with the top of the convertible down. "Do you still want to go to a movie?" Hunter asked.

"No," Elle said. "It's too nice out. Let's eat outside somewhere."

They stopped at a beachside café. Elle picked a table with a beautiful view of the night sky.

"How's school going?" Hunter asked.

"Great," Elle said. "The boys' basketball team's no good without you, though." The Killer Bees had won the championship the year before, with a little help from Elle, but mostly thanks to Hunter's great skill.

"We cheerleaders are trying to psych them up," she went on. "But I think the team misses your leadership."

"Can't win every year," Hunter said. "And how do you like being Ruler-of-All-You-Survey?"

Elle laughed. "If you mean student body president, it's great. Each class elected its student senators this year, and for once there were a lot of kids running for office. All of a sudden everybody wants to be in the student senate."

"You know why, don't you?" Hunter said. "It's because you're the president. You made student government cool."

"I thought it was because of the T-shirts," Elle said. She had designed T-shirts for every member of the student senate, complete with the senate logo—Senator Bee—in red, blue, and black. The shirt had become the cool fashion item of the season. "And the fact that I promised to bring homemade cookies to every meeting," she added.

"It's because people like you," Hunter said. "They want to be where you are."

He reached across the table and took Elle's hand. "I know I do," he added.

Elle felt flushed. Chessie was right—Hunter sure knew just what to say.

"What about you?" she asked him. "Are you used to being a college boy, now that you've made it through one semester?" The second semester of Hunter's freshman year had just begun.

"I guess," Hunter said. "I'm still so busy. I made the basketball squad, so that's good. But I've got so much schoolwork. I actually have to do some studying when I get back from dinner."

"You do?" Elle said. "But it's Saturday night! You have to study on Saturday nights?"

"Sometimes," Hunter said.

"I thought you'd go to frat parties and mixers and stuff like that in college."

"Sometimes we do that, too," Hunter said. "I've got a heavy course load this semester. Lots of lab work and research projects. Tons of reading. You'll see when you get to college. It's way tougher than high school."

After dinner they took a walk on the beach, hand in hand. They sat on a dune and kissed in the moonlight. Then Hunter squinted at his watch. "Whoops. I'd better get going if I'm going to finish my history reading by Monday."

"Don't you want to kiss some more?" Elle asked.

"Believe me, I'd much rather kiss you than read about the Teapot Dome scandal," Hunter said. "But life can't be *all* hearts and flowers."

"Why not?" Elle said, only half kidding.

He tousled her hair. "You're such a kid sometimes. That's what I like about you."

He kissed her one more time, then helped her to her feet. The air was cooler now, so they put the top up on the car and drove home. Elle was quiet.

Hunter pulled up in front of her house. "Can't

wait to see you next weekend," he said. He walked her to her door and kissed her one last time.

"Have a good week at school," Elle said.

"You, too," Hunter said.

She went inside and watched him walk back to his car. She could still feel his kiss, warm on her lips.

There's no problem with Hunter, she thought. *Everything is great between us.* He was still crazy about her. She could feel it. Chessie didn't know what she was talking about. Julia could never come between Elle and Hunter. Nobody could.

She wasn't worried. Not a bit.

Chapter 3

"I SAW JULIA yesterday," Chessie chirped after cheer-leading practice on Monday.

"So?" Laurette said. "Is that like seeing the Dalai Lama or something?"

Elle and Chessie had left the gym and bumped into Laurette, who was coming from a guitar lesson. The three of them walked across the school lawn together.

Elle heard a low toot and looked around. Sidney Ugman was running after them, hauling his French horn. "Wait up!"

"Oh, great," Chessie said. "Here comes Bologna Breath."

Sidney's family lived next door to Elle's. He'd

had a crush on her since kindergarten. It was unrequited and, as far as Elle was concerned, always would be. Still, she couldn't be mean to him. She couldn't be mean to anyone. That was probably why Sidney's crush had lasted so long.

Elle slowed down. Sidney finally caught up with the girls, out of breath.

"I'm glad I caught you," Sidney said. "You want a ride home?"

"No, thanks," Elle said. "I drove my own car to school today."

"Oh," Sidney said. "Well, can I come with you?"

Elle was confused. "But—you just offered me a ride."

"I can leave my car here overnight," Sidney said. "I won't need it until tomorrow morning."

"Then how will you get to school tomorrow, lamebrain?" Chessie said. She had no qualms about being mean to people she considered her social inferiors.

Sidney grinned at Elle. "Elle can give me a lift."

"But, if you have your own car," Elle said, "why not just drive yourself? It doesn't make any sense."

"Will you go out with me, then?" Sidney said.

Elle sighed. He asked her out every chance he

got. "I still have a boyfriend, Sidney. Just like I did when you asked me out yesterday."

"Things change," Sidney said. "You never know. Anything can happen. Even the happiest relationships can fall apart, just like *that*." He snapped his fingers.

"I hate to say it, but he's right, you know," Chessie said. "For once in his life."

"Well, as of now, I'm not free to go out with anyone," Elle said. "Thanks for asking."

"All right," Sidney said. "See you tomorrow. Unless you want to come over tonight and play Twister."

Elle tapped her book bag. "Too much homework."

"Right. Okay. See you!" Sidney walked off and disappeared in the school parking lot.

"Thank God he's gone," Chessie said. "I can breathe again!"

"The guy really does smell like bologna," Laurette said. "It's uncanny."

"So I was saying, I saw Julia yesterday," Chessie said.

"We know," Laurette said. "We heard you the first time."

Chessie ignored Laurette, as she often did. "She

stopped by her parents' house to pick up her National Honor Society pin," she said. "I guess her sorority wanted to see it or something. Normally she'd never mention it—she's not the type to brag."

"She made the National Honor Society?" Elle asked.

"She got a full scholarship to the college of her choice," Chesse said. "She's so smart! You don't meet a lot of girls who are model-beautiful and brilliant, too. I know it's a cliché, but it's true. Clichés are clichés for a reason, right?"

"Clichés?" What was Chessie talking about? Elle's head was spinning. Hunter hadn't mentioned all this about Julia. He hadn't mentioned her at all. Maybe he didn't know her that well.

"Of course, if she hadn't gotten a scholarship for brains, she would have gotten one for spring-board diving," Chessie said. "She's like, Olympic level, practically. She could have gone to the Olympics easily, but she decided to just be a normal person. A normal, brilliant, drop-dead gorgeous person. Who will inherit millions when her grand-father dies. He invented cement or something."

"Wow," Elle said. "She sounds like an interesting person to live next door to."

"She is," Chessie said. "But the main thing is

she's so totally nice. Like, *so* nice. She used to babysit me once in a while, and she always made homemade ice cream and let me stay up late with her. She's the coolest. You'd think she'd be stuck-up, but she isn't at all."

"She sounds nice," Elle said.

"She sounds totally made up," Laurette said.

"Do you think I'm exaggerating?" Chessie said. "I'm actually playing down all her good qualities."

"I don't think you're exaggerating," Laurette said. "I think you're lying."

Elle couldn't help feeling overwhelmed by all this information. If Julia was so incredible, what would stop Hunter from falling for her? But maybe she wouldn't like Hunter. No, that was impossible. Any girl, no matter how smart, talented, and gorgeous, would like Hunter.

"Maybe I'll meet her sometime," Elle said, "if Hunter becomes friends with her. Then the three of us can be friends."

"He already is friends with her," Chessie said. "She said they hang out all the time."

"Oh," Elle said. "That's nice."

"So how did Hunter like the Kappa party Saturday night?" Chessie said.

"Kappa party?" Elle said, a little confused.

"What are you talking about?"

"Julia's pledging this sorority called Kappa Kappa Gamma," Chessie said. "They had a big party Saturday night."

"Hunter didn't go," Elle said. "He went out with me."

"Really?" Chessie bit her lip. "That's funny."

"Why?" Elle said.

"Well . . . Julia said she saw Hunter there. But it was pretty late. It could have been after your date."

"You've been waiting all day for the right moment to bring this up," Laurette said, "haven't you? You're loving this."

"Stay out of this, Laurette," Chessie said. "It's no big deal, Elle. He probably just ditched you after your date got boring and then went to the party. Without you."

"But . . . he told me he had to study," Elle said.

Chessie shrugged. "Boys. What are you going to do?"

"Don't listen to her, Elle," Laurette said. "Darren tells me all about stuff like this." Her boyfriend, Darren Kidd, was a freshman in college, too, at UC Santa Barbara. "Lots of times he's on his way to the library, fully intending to study, when some friends of his waylay him and drag him off to a party somewhere. It happens all the time. It's the college way. It doesn't mean Hunter lied to you or didn't want to bring you. He was probably dragged there against his will."

"I'm sure the sorority girls held a gun to his head," Chessie said.

"You can't upset Elle, so stop trying," Laurette said. "She knows Hunter's crazy about her. She doesn't have to worry about a thing. Sure, he's in college and she's here, still stuck in boring old high school, but that's not the end of the world. She can't keep tabs on him every minute. She doesn't have to. She trusts him. Right, Elle?"

"Right," Elle said. "I'm sure Hunter got lots of studying done before he went to the party. What was he supposed to do, come to my house and pick me up again at midnight so I could go with him? That would be pretty silly."

"Very silly," Chessie said. "After all, he's already seeing you once a week, right? How much more could he take?"

Just then, Elle's cell phone jingled. She checked the caller ID. "It's Hunter," she said, stepping away for a little privacy.

"Hi, Buttercup," Hunter said. "How's your Monday?"

"Not bad," Elle said. "Mondayish."

"Listen, I've got some bad news. I can't make our date Friday night. I've got this huge sociology proposal due next Monday and I'm going to need all weekend to get it done. I've got a chemistry test Thursday, so I won't have a chance to work on this sociology project till that's over. I wanted to let you know as soon as possible so you could make other plans."

"Thanks," Elle said. "That's so thoughtful of you."

"I'm really sorry," Hunter said. "Believe me, I'd rather be out with you than cooped up in the stuffy old library any night. But if I miss the deadline, my whole semester will be ruined. You understand, don't you, Buttercup?"

"Of course, I do," Elle said. "Don't worry about it. School comes first."

"Actually, you come first," Hunter said. "School just gets in the way sometimes."

Elle smiled.

"I had a great time the other night," Hunter said. "Moonlight kisses are the best kind."

Elle stiffened. She thought about what Chessie had told her, about Julia saying she saw Hunter at her party. Should she ask him about it? Or would it sound bad, nagging, as if she didn't trust him?

"Elle?" he said. "Is everything okay?"

She couldn't help it. She had to ask.

"Sure," she said. "Chessie was just telling me that this girl Julia is in a couple of your classes. She's Chessie's neighbor. Do you know her?"

"Julia? You mean, Julia Gables? Sure I know her. She's a great girl."

She would rather have heard him say, *She's a troll*, but that wouldn't be like Hunter. At least he didn't sound nervous talking about her. Or guilty.

She pressed on. "Chessie said that Julia said that you went to a sorority party on Saturday night. But I told her that was impossible because you were with me. And then you were studying. Right?"

"Actually, I finished studying around midnight and went out for a snack," Hunter said. "The party was still raging, so I stopped by. Said hello to a few people, then back to the dorm. I was pretty tired. Why? Are you worried about it?"

"No." Elle felt better now. "Not at all." He had just stopped by and said hello to a few people. That was no crime. Campus life was like that. At least, she imagined it was. As Laurette said, it was the college way.

"I'm sorry about this weekend," Hunter said again. "I'll make it up to you somehow. I'll call you tonight after I get back from the library, okay?"

"Okay," Elle said.

"Are you still my buttercup?" Hunter said.

"Always," Elle said.

She clicked off.

"So?" Chessie asked. "What did he want?"

"As if it's any of your business," Laurette said.

"Elle doesn't have to tell me if she doesn't want to," Chessie said.

"It's nothing," Elle said. "He canceled our date this weekend. Some big project is due."

"That's all right, Elle," Laurette said. "You and I will do something fun together."

"Isn't that funny?" Chessie said. "He bailed on Homecoming because of a big school project, too. Or so he said."

"What's so funny about that?" Laurette asked.

Chessie shrugged. "It's the same excuse, twice in a row. I'm just saying."

"Of course, it is," Laurette said. "The guy's in *college*. The whole point is to study. He's swamped with work. Right, Elle?"

"It's true," Elle said. "He really does have a project."

"So you believe him?" Chessie said.

"Totally," Elle said.

Chapter 4

"I SWEAR, UNDERDOG gets cuter every week. Just like his mama." Bibi Barbosa, Elle's hairstylist, manicurist, and all-around advice guru, scratched Underdog between the ears. Her own Chihuahua, Kitty, was Underdog's mother.

"It's true. He's a doll." Elle gave Underdog a squeeze before setting him down in the basket Bibi kept at the Pamperella Salon just for him. He snuggled up against Kitty, who licked him. Elle and Underdog saw Bibi and Kitty at least once a week for a manicure and problem-solving session.

"What'll it be today, hon?" Bibi asked in her Texas twang. She took off her cowboy hat and tossed her long brown hair over her shoulder.

The salon was bustling, as usual. "I'm tired of this funky purple nail polish," she said, glancing at Elle's nails. "Let's go for a nice true red. What do you say?"

"Sounds good," Elle said. "I've been wearing a lot of red lately."

"For Valentine's Day, am I right?" Bibi said. "To get yourself in the mood? What kind of plans do you and Hunter have?"

"I haven't said anything to him yet," Elle said. "But I wanted to surprise him with a special dinner at my house, by the pool."

"Sounds romantic," Bibi said. "Have you been sticking to your once-a-week date schedule?"

Once-a-week date schedule. That sounded so *un*romantic. More like tutoring. "Sort of," Elle said. "Hunter had to cancel this week. Some big school project."

"That's a shame," Bibi said. "You must be disappointed."

"I am," Elle said. "But Laurette and I are going to do something fun together instead. We don't need boys around to have a good time."

"Heck, no," Bibi said. "Sometimes having boys around spoils the fun!" She gently set down Elle's left hand, now free of purple nail polish, and picked up the right one. "You're not upset about him canceling, are you?"

"No," Elle said. "Do you think I should be?"

"No," Bibi said. She looked at Elle. Elle looked down at her hands. Bibi could always tell when something was bothering her.

"Spill it," Bibi said.

"It's nothing, really," Elle said. "It's just that after our last date, he told me he was going back to campus to study, but then Chessie said she heard he was at a party that night."

"Hold it right there," Bibi said. "I see two problems here. Number one: Chessie. You know how she operates. She loves to make you feel insecure."

"No, she doesn't." Bibi and Laurette had been saying that to Elle all year, but she refused to believe it. Why would someone want to undermine someone else? It didn't make sense to her. "She just doesn't know how to express herself well. She's awkward. Things come out in ways she doesn't mean them."

Bibi shook her head. "Oh, Elle. All right, forget Chessie. Number two: Hunter. He's one of the good ones. You can see it in his face. You don't have to worry about him, Elle."

"I know that," Elle said. "It's just hard, with him

being in a different school and everything, and so busy. We never get to see each other, and then he cancels . . ."

"That is hard," Bibi said. "But you'll get through it. Meantime, you get to go out for a whoop-de-do girl night with your best friend, Laurette. Nothing wrong with that."

Elle smiled. Bibi always knew how to make her feel better. The hand massage and fresh coat of nail polish didn't hurt, either.

"What do you think Darren is doing right now?" Elle asked. She and Laurette left the movie theater and headed down the street to their favorite gelato shop. It was Saturday night, and Santa Monica Boulevard was crowded with people.

"He's probably practicing with his new band," Laurette said. Darren played electric guitar and wanted to be a rock star. "I bet he's yelling at his drummer right now to quit fooling around and keep the beat steady for once. He can get pretty grumpy at band practice."

"You should know," Elle said. Laurette had learned to play guitar the previous summer and had played with Darren's old band, Warp Factor 5, a few times.

"What do you think Hunter's doing?" Laurette asked.

Elle shrugged. "Huddled at a desk in the library, I guess. Or stuck in his room, staring out the window while everyone else on campus parties."

"Too bad they're not having fun, like we are," Laurette said. "Suckers."

They walked into the gelato shop and ordered some ice cream. They sat outside on a bench to eat it. When they were finished, Elle didn't know what to do next. It was only nine o'clock.

"Want to go to your house and play Scrabble?" she asked. She and Laurette liked to play Scrabble with Laurette's mother, Margarita.

"Mom's got a date," Laurette said. "She's making dinner for him. I'd rather not go home until he's gone. You know. It gets awkward."

"Gotcha," Elle said. "How about my house? My parents went out to dinner. Hey, there they are now."

Elle's parents, Eva and Wyatt Woods, got out of their Jaguar in front of Delissima, the restaurant next door. Wyatt handed his car keys to the valet. Eva spotted the girls on their bench and waved.

"Here they come," Elle said. Eva clicked along the sidewalk in her high heels, followed by Wyatt.

They were both tanned, glowing, well-groomed, and perfectly dressed.

"How was the movie, girls?" Wyatt asked.

"Funny," Elle said.

"Do you miss your boyfriends tonight?" Eva asked.

"No," Laurette said emphatically.

"Good for you," Wyatt said.

"Well, *I* miss Hunter," Eva said. "If I don't get my weekly Hunter fix, I feel as if something's missing."

Wyatt shook his head. "You don't want him to flunk out of college just to please you, do you?"

"Of course not," Eva said, "but he should make more time for me and Elle."

"What are you doing now, girls?" Wyatt asked.

"We don't know," Elle said.

"Zosia was looking bored when we left," Eva said. "Apparently her date stood her up, too."

"Mom, nobody stood us up," Elle said.

"Of course, dear," Eva said. "Anyway, I'm sure she'd love some company."

"We'd better go, darling," Wyatt said. "We're late for our dinner reservation."

"Have fun, girls!" Eva said as they trotted back to the restaurant.

Elle looked at Laurette. "We could watch a movie with Zosia," she said.

"Sounds good to me," Laurette said.

They drove to Elle's house. Zosia seemed happy to see them. Bernard offered to make caramel popcorn, which they accepted, even though they were full.

Elle stopped in her room to check her e-mail. "Hurry up, Elle!" Zosia called from the living room. "The movie is about to start."

"I'll be right there," Elle said. She had no new e-mails. No voice messages on her cell. Still, she thought she'd give Hunter a quick call to cheer him up.

She dialed his number. His voice mail picked up right away. *He must have turned his phone off so he could concentrate*, she thought. She left him a quick, cheerful message.

After the movie, Laurette decided to sleep over. "That way there's zero chance of running into Mom's date," she said. After midnight, their stomachs full of caramel popcorn, the girls got changed into pajamas (Laurette borrowed a pair). Before they got into bed, Elle checked her voice mail one more time. No messages.

"He's probably still at the library," Laurette said.

"I know," Elle said. "I just wish he'd call anyway."

"How was your weekend?" Hunter asked when he finally called her on Monday morning.

"Okay," Elle said. "How was yours? Did you finish your project?"

"We're just getting started," Hunter said. "But our proposal was due today, and that's all finished. I think we polished it up into pretty good shape. We sure worked hard."

"We?" Elle said.

"Me and Julia," Hunter said. "We're doing a big sociology project together. She's my partner. For the semester."

The bottom dropped out of Elle's stomach. "She is? Julia Gables, you mean?"

"That's right. She's the one whose parents live next door to Chessie, remember?"

"Uh-huh," Elle said. "So you were working with her, just the two of you? All weekend?"

"It was a lot of work," Hunter said. "We're just learning how to write these project proposals. The professor won't let you start your project until he approves it. It's a pretty big deal."

Elle swallowed. "Well, I hope you get an A."

"Thanks," Hunter said. "I sure missed you, though. Have a good day at school, and I'll talk to you later."

Elle hung up and sat on the bed. Hunter had canceled his date with her to spend the whole weekend with Julia. Elle knew they were studying, but this was only the beginning. They'd be doing a project together all semester. Four whole months.

How can I compete with that? Elle thought. *Julia's on campus with Hunter twenty-four hours a day—and I get to see him one night a week, if I'm lucky!*

It wasn't fair. It just wasn't.

Chapter 5

"I DON'T SEE what you're so worried about, Elle," Chessie said at school later that morning. "I asked Julia if Hunter had mentioned you, and she said your name didn't sound familiar. So it's not as if he's bad-mouthing you to her or anything."

"Why would Hunter bad-mouth Elle?" Laurette snapped.

Elle hadn't even thought of that. "You mean, Hunter hasn't told her he has a girlfriend yet?"

Chessie shrugged. "Guess not."

Laurette gave Chessie the evil eye. "Probably because all they talk about is schoolwork, not personal stuff. Which makes sense, since there's nothing romantic going on."

"Or he wants Julia to think he's available," Chessie said.

Elle felt the blood drain from her face.

"I'm just saying," Chessie said.

"Keep your comments to yourself, Chessie," Laurette said. "You're no help at all."

Elle was a wreck for the rest of the day. She could hardly concentrate in class. That afternoon she canceled her senate meeting and had Chloe take over for her at cheerleading practice.

She called Bibi for an emergency appointment. "It's Elle," she said. "Do you have any free time today?"

"Well—" Bibi hesitated, which wasn't like her at all. "Things are a little bit crazy here—"

"Please," Elle said. "I have to see you right away."

"Sure, honey," Bibi said. "Come on over."

Bibi's voice sounded funny over the phone, but Elle didn't give it much thought. Bad connection, probably.

Elle jumped into her car and hurried over to Rodeo Drive. She parked right in front of Pamperella. There was some kind of commotion going on across the street, but Elle didn't take much notice. She didn't need any commotion in her life at the moment. She needed help.

She walked into Pamperella. The usually bustling salon was oddly quiet.

Where is everybody? Elle thought. Must be a slow day.

She found Bibi at her station, slumped in her own styling chair. She straightened up when she saw Elle.

"Something's wrong," Bibi said, grabbing Elle's hand and studying her nails. "I just gave you a manicure a few days ago, and your nails are fine. Your hair is fine. This is a personal visit. Am I right?"

"Right," Elle said.

"Pull up a chair," Bibi said.

Elle collapsed into the chair next to Bibi's. She looked around. Where was the receptionist? Where were all the other stylists?

"Is it about Hunter?" Bibi asked.

"Yes," Elle said, and she spilled out the whole story. "He canceled our date to study with Julia. All weekend long. *Now* should I be worried?"

"I need a minute to let this sink in," Bibi said. She tapped an emery board on the arm of her chair. Elle couldn't help noticing the quiet again. No blow-dryers blowing, no voices chattering, no groovy dance beats coming from the stereo . . .

"You know what?" Bibi said at last. "I'm going to have to stick with what I said before. I agree, this situation doesn't sound ideal, but I don't see what you can do about it. You can't ask the guy to drop out of school, right? And you wouldn't want to. Hunter's a good guy. I don't think he's cheating on you. All you can do is trust him."

"Okay," Elle said. But she felt unsatisfied. She wasn't getting the warm, comforting feeling she usually got after a Bibi session. And Bibi looked very worried. She had dark circles under her eyes, which she hadn't bothered to cover with concealer. Very unlike her.

Something was wrong.

"Why is it so quiet in here?" Elle asked. "Where is everybody?"

"Didn't you see?" Bibi said, nodding toward the front door. "Across the street?"

Elle got up and went to the door. The crowd across the street was even bigger than before. It looked like the grand opening of some kind of new store. But why would that affect Pamperella's business?

"What is that place?" Elle asked. "Are they having some kind of supersale or something? Is that where everybody is?"

"They're not having a supersale," Bibi said. "It's a new salon. Vernay."

"Huh," Elle said. "Well, I still don't see—"

"Vernay, as in Valerie Vernay," Bibi said. "Stylist to the stars? Creator of the 'Val,' that haircut made famous by Tippi Hanover, super-mega-über teen star?"

"Oh, yeah," Elle said. "A girl on my cheerleading squad just got one of those."

"Everybody in town wants a Val," Bibi said. "Valerie Vernay is superhot. She's becoming more famous than the stars she works on. Most of our regular customers canceled their appointments today. The other stylists didn't even bother to come in. Everybody's over there, trying to buy a few minutes of Valerie's time."

"But your customers are so loyal," Elle said. "They love you."

Bibi looked sad. "It's hard to compete against the hot new thing. But why did she have to open her new salon right across the street from us? She's luring all our business away."

"It's probably just a fad," Elle said. "Your customers will come back. Nobody offers quality and value like you do, along with that personal touch."

"I hope you're right," Bibi said, "because if they

don't come back soon, I'm in big trouble. Pamperella will close. I'll lose my job. And then what will I do? I'll have to go back to Texas!"

"No!" Elle cried. "You can't leave town!"

This was terrible! Elle felt as if her whole life were crumbling. How could she lose Hunter and Bibi, too?

"I won't let that happen," Elle said. "There's got to be a way to save Pamperella."

"I don't know," Bibi said. "I've seen this happen before. A cute new kitty comes along and suddenly the old cat doesn't look so good anymore."

"That won't happen to you," Elle said. "People always need good styling and TLC. It never goes out of style."

"But haircuts do," Bibi said. "And how can I compete with Valerie? With someone who's on *Entertainment Tonight* every week? Someone who's a red-carpet style commentator for the Oscars? Compared to her, I'm just a nobody."

"I've got it," Elle said. "You'll become a celebrity stylist, too! You're good enough. You're the best stylist in L.A. All you need are some famous clients and lots of press coverage."

"That sounds great," Bibi said. "But how do we do that? How do we get famous clients when every celebrity in town has sworn lifelong allegiance to Valerie?"

"I'll come up with something," Elle said. "Don't worry. Whatever you do, don't let the salon close!"

"I'll try my best," Bibi said. "Thanks, Elle."

But she didn't seem very cheered up. And neither did Elle. They both sat slumped in their chairs, brooding over their troubles.

I've got to fix this, Elle thought. *What would I do without Bibi? And Hunter? My whole world would implode!*

The trouble was, from where she was sitting, her problems looked impossible to solve. That wouldn't stop her from trying. But it would be nice to have a few ideas. . . .

Chapter 6

ELLE SAT ON A STOOL near the stove, stirring a pot of boiling sugar water. Bernard stood nearby, supervising. Zosia sat at the kitchen table, cutting flowers.

"Keep stirring, keep stirring . . ." Bernard said.

Bernard had been teaching Elle to cook and bake, and the more she did it, the more she liked it. It was soothing. When she was troubled, baking a cake or stir-frying some vegetables helped her feel better.

Eva flounced in, waving a copy of *People*. "Big news!" she said. "Guess who's got a hair appointment with *Valerie Vernay?*"

Elle's heart sank. "You?" she guessed.

"Correct," Eva said. She opened the magazine

and flashed a picture of Valerie posing arm in arm with Tippi Hanover. "Of course, I had to pull a few strings. Those appointments are impossible to get. But luckily your father is the most sought-after plastic surgeon in town, and when I dropped his name and told Valerie's receptionist he'd give her a consultation . . ."

Elle dropped her spoon on the counter. "Mom, that's terrible! Valerie Vernay is stealing all of Pamperella's business. Bibi's customers have deserted her. She might have to move back to Texas!"

"Keep stirring, Elle," Bernard said. "You don't want the sugar to burn."

Elle picked up her spoon and stirred vigorously.

"That's a shame," Eva said. "But the Val is the hottest thing in Hollywood. I've got to have one." She paused and watched as Elle beat the sugar with her spoon. "What are you doing?"

"I'm making candy hearts," Elle said. "It's practice for the big show. Valentine's Day."

"Elle's going to give out candy with special personalized messages, just for her school," Bernard said. "This is the trial run."

"I'm bringing them in to the senate meeting tomorrow to see what everybody thinks," Elle said.

"I'm planning the biggest Valentine's Day celebration Beverly Hills High has ever seen. A daylong party for the whole school, with special food at lunch, and decorations, love songs over the intercom, romantic movies, class parties . . . and whatever else people can think up."

The idea had come to her after talking to her friends who didn't have dates. Why shouldn't everybody have a good time, anyway? she'd thought.

"That sounds lovely, dear," Eva said. "But can't you just *buy* some candy hearts?"

"These are going to be special," Elle said. They'll say *BEE My Valentine*, because our team is the Bees, you know, and *BHH Is for Lovers*, and stuff like that."

Eva shook her head. "You certainly do work hard. Which makes me feel funny about my next question, but I'll ask it anyway. Do you think you could help out at the gallery tomorrow afternoon? Zenobia has the flu, and I've got an appointment with my aura reader. . . ."

Eva owned an art gallery called, appropriately enough, the Eva Woods Gallery, and she had a big show of paintings running. Elle looked up from her stirring.

"I can't. I've got a student senate meeting

tomorrow afternoon, and I have to go," she said. "But I promise to help out after school on Wednesday."

"All right, sweetie," Eva said. "I understand."

"I'll help out, Mrs. Woods," Zosia said.

"Would you, Zosia? That would be perfect," Eva said. "Bye, honey. I have to run." She hurried away before Elle could say another word.

"You can't blame your mother for wanting a Val," Zosia said. "She's a creature of fashion. If she can't have the latest hairstyle, she might as well crawl into a hole and die."

Elle sighed. She knew it was true. Her mother was a slave to the latest trends, and moral implications never factored into it.

"Order! Order!" Instead of banging a gavel to get the student senators' attention, Elle squeezed one of Underdog's toys, a squeaky rubber steak. She was thinking she'd need to find something louder.

"So, we all agree that our newly appointed school DJ, Cassie, should play dance music in the halls every Friday afternoon to pump up the jam." Elle nodded at a small, redheaded girl who represented the tenth grade. Cassie Meeks bounced in her seat with excitement. "But we can't agree on the first song. I say we leave it to Cassie. Agreed?"

"Definitely not," Dolores Stanley said. "Her taste is way too metal." Dolores scratched her pierced nose with a long black fingernail. She was more into Goth.

"We can't fight about this forever," Will Campbell said. He was a senior senator with shaggy light brown hair. He had to wear glasses for reading, which Elle thought was cute. "As long as Cassie agrees to play a variety of music, there will be plenty of time for all kinds of songs."

Elle smiled gratefully at Will. He was turning out to be her biggest ally and helper in keeping the peace. Senate meetings were lively, and sometimes the discussions got out of hand.

Still, the senate was fun. Elle had spruced up the meeting room, transforming it from a boring classroom into a groovy lounge, with beanbag chairs; couches; curtains; a TV for video presentations, should anyone have to make one; and a music system.

Her own seat—a gift from the cheerleading squad—was called the Speaker's Throne: a padded, high-backed wooden chair painted gold and topped with a wooden crown. She brought sandwiches, cookies, and iced tea to every meeting and always wore her pink STUDENT SENATE T-shirt. The student senate was now one of the coolest extra-curricular activities at BHH. Every meeting was like a party.

"Okay," Elle said. "Let's break up into subcommittees. The music committee, party committee, and gossip committee—gather over by the yoga mats. The beach committee, fashion committee, and fortune-telling committee—take the Ouija board table. The Valentine's Day committee will stay here by the Speaker's Throne."

Elle and Will were cochairs of the Valentine's Day committee, her pet project.

"Okay, do we have permission from the cafeteria for the special Valentine's Day lunch?" Elle asked.

Will checked his notes. "Yep. They agreed to heart-shaped minipizzas, beet salad, strawberry cupcakes, and chocolate kisses at every table. They vetoed the oysters, though."

"That's all right," Elle said. "I knew oysters were a long shot. Good. Okay, Cassie's handling the music, nothing but love songs, over the intercom all day. Craig, what movies have you picked out?"

Craig Jenkins was in charge of showing romantic movies in the auditorium. Not because he was particularly romantic, but because he knew how to run a projector.

"I've got *Casablanca*, *Sleepless in Seattle*, *Ghost*, *Titanic*, *Breakfast at Tiffany's*, *The Princess Bride*, *Love Story*, *Romeo and Juliet*, and *Speed*."

"*Speed*? Is that a romantic movie?" Elle asked. She thought she'd seen it on cable one night. "Isn't that the movie about the bus that can't stop?"

Craig nodded. "It's my all-time favorite."

"I think we'll have to take it off the list," Elle said. "A girl and her bus . . . It's not quite romantic enough." Craig looked disappointed, so Elle added, "Don't worry, we'll play it on another holiday, like, maybe, National Transportation Day or something. Good job, Craig."

"What's left, Chief?" Will asked.

"Decorations," Elle said. "My department. I'm making lots of big cutout hearts, red and white streamers, that kind of thing. Anybody want to volunteer to help me? I've designed and drawn everything. I just need help with cutting and gluing."

"I will," Will said.

"Great," Elle said. "Thanks. When Valentine's Day gets closer, you can come over to my house and we'll get to work. In the meantime, I'll send out a schoolwide e-mail to all students and faculty to remember to wear red, white, and pink that day. Silver and gold are also acceptable."

"There's only one problem," Will said. "This party is going to cost money."

"You're right," Elle said. "The food, the art supplies, the metallic paint. How much do we have in the budget?"

Will checked the ledger. "Not much. We depleted the budget with the holiday party."

"I see," Elle said. "Well, we'll just have to figure out a way to raise some money, fast. We don't need a whole lot. . . ."

"We could make a record," Craig said. "Like they do in England when they want to help starving people. 'Valentine Aid. The Beverly Hills Student Senate Sings Love Songs.'"

"Yeah!" Elle loved that idea. "Accompanied by the Beverly Hills Marching Band!"

Will wrinkled his nose. "I don't know," he said. "Most of the student senators are not good singers. If they were, they'd probably be in the chorus."

"That's true," Elle said.

"There must be an easier way," Will said.

Craig dipped into the bowl of Elle's special Valentine's Day hearts. "This candy is good," he said. He read the message on the heart he'd chosen—U R 2 TAN—and laughed. "And funny."

"Why don't we sell your candy to the people in the neighborhood?" Will suggested. "You've made more than we can eat."

"We could wrap them up in pretty little boxes and sell them as Valentine's Day gifts," Elle said. "That's a great idea."

"You could get the cheerleaders to go from door to door in their uniforms," Craig said. "Like funky Girl Scouts."

"Even better," Elle said. "Okay, guess that's it. See you all next week."

The meeting broke up. Will and Elle walked out into the hallway together.

"Another great session, Chief," Will said. "School senate is way more fun since you became the prez."

"Thanks, Will." Elle was pleased. Doing a good job as president meant a lot to her, since, when she first announced her candidacy, most people had laughed at the idea.

"I mean it," Will said. "You've got this way about you. . . . It's like magic. You bring people together."

Elle blushed. She didn't know what to say. Luckily, she didn't have to say anything. Laurette came out of the school-newspaper office and walked toward them.

"Fancy meeting you here," Laurette said. "Guess what? I'm going to be a reporter for the paper."

"Excellent," Elle said. "You can plant stories for me. I need a big buildup for Valentine's Day."

"It's going to be boffo," Will said. "See you tomorrow, Elle."

"See you."

Will turned a corner. Elle and Laurette continued on to their lockers.

"Will has a crush on you," Laurette said in a singsongy voice.

"No, he doesn't," Elle said.

"He *so* does," Laurette said. "It's totally obvious. Don't you see how he looks at you?"

"He's just very serious about the student senate," Elle said.

"Sure he is," Laurette said. "And he's supercute, too. I like his little glasses."

"We're just friends," Elle said.

"I know," Laurette said. "I'm just calling it like I see it."

"I'm in love with Hunter," Elle said.

"I know that," Laurette said. "How could I not? I'm just saying, it's not *impossible* that you could date Hunter *and* Will. You're not married to the guy. Yet."

"I know," Elle said. "But I'm a one-boy girl. I can't imagine kissing anybody but Hunter."

Chapter 7

"FIRST WE'LL PAINT our special love messages on the hearts," Elle explained. She'd invited the cheerleading squad to her house to make more valentine candy. "Then we'll wrap them up in these little red heart-shaped boxes. Be sure to tie the ribbon in a nice big bow, like this." Elle demonstrated how to tie up the boxes.

"We'll sell them for five dollars each," Laurette said. She'd come along to help out. "That should make plenty of money to buy what we need for the party."

"Some of the herbs in Zosia's love potion are expensive, even when you buy them in bulk," Elle said.

"And we can paint any message we want on the candy?" Chessie asked.

"Not *any* message," Elle said. "It has to be Valentine-appropriate."

She had spread out trays of freshly made candy hearts all over the kitchen. Each girl had an ultra-thin paintbrush and food coloring to decorate the hearts with.

Elle diligently painted romantic messages on her hearts and outlined each one in red or pink. I ❤ U; B MY BF; LET'S POWWOW; I WANT UR DIGITZ; OUQT INVU . . .

Then she walked around the room to see what the other girls were writing.

"I'm doing the Hipster Series," Laurette said, showing off her work. Her hearts said I DIG U; MOPTOP; and IN-D RAWK 4-EVER.

"Excellent," Elle said. "I'm sure there's a market for those."

"In the thrift-store district," Chessie said. "Try Los Feliz or Silverlake. Not the Hills."

"Money's money," Laurette said. "Whether it comes from Silverlake or the 3 Bs." Which, everyone knew, stood for Beverly Hills, Brentwood, and Bel Air.

Chessie scoffed. "They don't have money in

Silverlake. Not *real* money."

"I'm sure they pay for their lattes with something," Elle said. "Let's see what you've written, Chessie."

The other girls had written BEVHILLS HOT-T; I M POSTAL 4U; BIG UPS; SNAPS; U R A BETTY; WHATEV . . .

"Everybody's writing nice, lovey-dovey slogans," Chessie said. "I think we need to balance those out with a few mean ones. There are always some mean hearts in the boxes you buy at the candy store."

"That's true," P.J. said.

"So I'm doing 2 PALE; TRY BOTOX; SPRAY TAN; and my masterpiece, UR FACELIFT IS DIVINE."

"How can you fit all that on one tiny heart?" Elle asked.

"I put it on four hearts," Chessie explained. "It's a series."

In response, Laurette picked up one of Chloe's hearts and gave it to Chessie. "Whatev."

"Let's wrap these up," Elle said. "And start selling!"

Elle gave each pair of cheerleaders a different route through the 3 Bs. "Remember," she said. "Spirit!"

She teamed up with Laurette, who stuck out a

little because she refused to wear a cheerleader uniform, even for one afternoon. And no one wanted to be with Chessie, so she was left without a partner. Over Laurette's protests, Elle took pity on Chessie and invited her to cover Brentwood with them.

They started at the house next door to Elle's. "This should be an easy sale," Laurette said. It was Sidney Ugman's house.

Elle pressed the doorbell. *Ding-dong, ding-dong . . . ding-dong, ding-dong . . .* it chimed.

A maid answered the door. "Hello, Elle," she said.

"Hello, Frida," Elle said. "We're selling candy hearts to raise money for a school Valentine's Day party. Would you like to buy some?"

"I'll handle this, Frida." Sidney appeared at the door in a velvet smoking jacket, a bubble-gum cigar stuck between his teeth. "Hello, ladies."

"Suave," Laurette said.

"Would you like to buy some candy, Sidney?" Elle asked.

"Most definitely," Sidney said. "I'll take three boxes."

"Great," Elle said. "That will be fifteen dollars."

Sidney reached into the pocket of his jacket. "Can you break a hundred?"

"No," Laurette said. "We don't have much change. This is the first house we stopped at."

"You don't have anything smaller?" Chessie said.

Sidney sighed. "Frida, can I borrow twenty dollars?"

"Jeez, borrowing money from his maid," Laurette said. "That's low."

Frida reappeared with a twenty-dollar bill. "Here you go, ladies," Sidney said. "Keep the change."

"Thanks." Elle gave him three boxes of candy hearts. Sidney gave one to Frida.

"For you," he said.

"Gee, thanks," Frida said. "This will really lighten my mood while I take your Kim Possible bedsheets out of the dryer." She took the box and disappeared into the kitchen.

Sidney nervously adjusted the belt of his smoking jacket. "She's kidding. She loves to tease me."

"Sure she does," Laurette said. "I bet you really sleep on Barney sheets."

Chessie laughed. "I don't normally like you, Laurette, but sometimes you can be really funny."

"I don't normally like you, either," Laurette said. "At least we agree on something."

"What are you going to do with the other two boxes, Sidney?" Elle asked.

Sidney put one away in his pocket. "I'll give one to Mother. And one is for you, Elle. An early Valentine's Day gift. With the promise of more to come, if you play your cards right."

He returned one box of candy to Elle. She took it and stared at it, not sure what to do.

"Ewww." Laurette grabbed it and put it back with the others to be resold. "We appreciate your contribution, Sidney," she said. "See you!"

"Don't you have any cute neighbors, Elle?" Chessie asked as they walked to the next house. "Maybe one of them will buy a box of candy for me. But he has to be cute."

"We're not here to meet boys," Laurette said. "We're supposed to be raising money."

They rang the doorbell of the next house. A thin, elegant middle-aged woman answered the door. She wore a terry-cloth beach cover-up, a sun hat, and sunglasses and carried a neon green frozen drink in her hand.

"Yes?"

Elle explained their mission.

"You poor girls," the woman said in a throaty voice. "You still believe in love and romance, don't you? How bittersweet to be young."

"Does that mean you don't want to buy any of

the candy we have for sale?" Laurette said.

"I don't believe in love anymore," the woman said, "so what would I do with candy hearts?"

"They're not all about love," Elle said. "Show her your masterpiece, Chessie."

Chessie opened a box of candy and picked through them until she found the four hearts she was looking for. "It's a four-part series." She lined them up and held them in her palm. UR FACELIFT IS DIVINE.

The woman gasped. Then she laughed and touched her cheek. "Why, thank you."

"We've also got CPA 2 THE STARS; I [HEART] MY BMW; and 90210=$$$," Elle said. She was glad that Chessie had made her own special hearts for the cynical crowd. A sale was a sale, no matter how unromantic. It would all go toward the super-romantic Valentine's Day party, so love would win in the end.

"I'll take two boxes," the woman said.

They sold candy at five of the next seven homes. "This is so easy," Chessie said. "I think I'll do this every week, to supplement my allowance."

They had gone beyond Elle's block now, and were in a part of the neighborhood she didn't know very well. They stopped at an iron gate that guarded a large green lawn leading to a brick mansion with white pillars.

"I wonder who lives here," Laurette said.

They buzzed the button on the gate. A voice spoke through the intercom: *"Who is it?"*

"I'm your neighbor, Elle Woods," Elle said. "I'm raising money for BHH. Would you like to buy some homemade Valentine's candy?"

The girls waited for an answer. The intercom was silent. It was as if someone were consulting with someone else about whether or not to let the girls in.

At last the intercom voice said, *"Come in."* The gate buzzed, and Elle pushed it open.

"This house looks familiar," Laurette said.

"Yeah," Chessie said. "And not just because it's in our neighborhood."

"I know," Elle said. "I saw it on *CrashPadz!*" *CrashPadz* was a show about houses of the rich and famous. "Do you know who lives here?"

"Who?" Laurette said.

"Marielle Stone and Richie Webb," Elle said.

Laurette and Chessie stopped in their tracks. Marielle Stone and Richie Webb were huge movie stars. They were married, but lately the tabloids had been saying that their marriage was on the rocks.

"She has a shoe closet in every room," Elle said. "Even the kitchen. Her shoe closet has a shoe closet. And she still doesn't have enough space for all her shoes. She's thinking of building a shoe house out back behind the pool."

"I read she's cheating on Richie with Noah Paxton," Chessie whispered. Noah Paxton was a hot young actor, very good-looking.

"I read he's cheating on Marielle with Tippi Hanover's mother," Laurette said.

Across the lawn, the front door opened. Elle gripped Laurette's hand.

"Come on," she said. "Let's go sell some candy."

A beautiful young woman with gold-flecked brown hair stood at the door in cutoff shorts and a T-shirt. Just behind her stood a gorgeous guy in surf shorts, with sunglasses hiding his famous sea-blue eyes. He wore flip-flops. The woman was barefoot.

Elle would have known them anywhere. For a while, she had watched Marielle's hit show, *Buddies*, every week. And she'd had a crush on Richie since junior high. But she tried to play it cool.

"We're waiting for our diet lunch to be delivered," Marielle said. "So we're starving."

"We're not supposed to have candy," Richie said.

"It serves those Malibu Diet jerks right for being late with our lunches," Marielle said. "It's their fault if I gain weight because of this."

"You're the one who wanted to go on the Malibu Diet," Richie snapped.

"You're the one who needs to lose ten pounds," Marielle said.

"I don't think either of you needs to lose any weight," Elle said. "You're gorgeous."

Both stars grinned. "You're a good salesgirl," Marielle said. "What kind of candy have you got?"

"Custom-made Valentine's Day hearts," Elle said, opening a box to show them. "Five dollars a box. Perfect for putting a little romance into your life."

Richie picked out a heart and read it. "I [HEART] $$$? That's not very romantic."

Elle frowned. "You got a Chessie box. Those are for nonlovers."

"That's not true," Chessie said. "They're for people who love money. That's a *form* of love."

"Amen, sister," Marielle said.

"Marielle should know," Richie said. "She'll do anything for money—right, honey?"

"At least I never played a surfing gorilla," Marielle said.

"Neither did I," Richie said.

"He's lying, girls," Marielle said. "You know that old surf movie *Big Kahuna*? Richie played the surfing gorilla. You can't see him because of the costume, but you can tell it's him by the terrible acting. His trademark."

"Marielle, you promised you'd never tell," Richie said.

"And *you* promised to love, honor, and cherish me till death do us part," Marielle said. "Not until the first hot starlet saunters by."

"Hey, I'm not the one who asks for head shots when hiring a pool boy," Richie said.

Elle glanced at Laurette and Chessie, feeling uncomfortable. This was getting out of control. She picked out a couple of hearts with nice sayings on them.

"Here, have a free sample." She gave Marielle and Richie each a heart.

Marielle read her heart. "It says, H-WOOD HUNK. This is for you, Rich."

"Thanks. Mine says, MY Q-T," Richie said. "From me to you, my cutie."

"Aw. Let's see what else is in here." Marielle took the box of candy from Elle and started digging through it. "Look! B MINE. Short, simple, and sweet—a classic. Will you be mine, Richie?"

He opened his mouth, and she fed him the heart. Then he gave her one that said, SUPERSTAR.

"We'll take two boxes," Marielle said.

"I'll go get some money," Richie said.

"Hurry back, Hollywood Hunk," Marielle said.

Elle made sure to give them only boxes of candy with nice sayings so they wouldn't start fighting again.

"I think we saved a Hollywood marriage in trouble," Laurette said as the girls were buzzed out.

"We should call the *National Enquirer* and tell them all about it," Chessie said. "Think how much we could get for the gorilla-suit scoop."

"Leave them alone," Elle said. "Our candy hearts are going out into the world, doing their good work. By Valentine's Day, the 3 Bs will be buzzing with love!"

Laurette shook her head in admiration. "Knowing you, they will be. Elle Woods, you're the only person I know who could pull it off."

Chapter 8

"WHAT'S THIS FOR?" Elle asked.

Hunter presented Elle with a small box wrapped in silver paper. It was Saturday night, the night of their weekly date. This week he hadn't canceled. He took Elle to a club near his campus, where a band was playing. They listened to the music and danced until they were dripping with sweat.

When the band finished playing, they left the club and stopped at a diner for milk shakes. That was when Hunter gave Elle the box.

"It's nothing," Hunter said. "I just wanted to make sure you knew how sorry I was about canceling last weekend. I hated to do it. . . ."

"But you've already apologized a dozen times,"

Elle said. "I know you're busy. You don't have to do this."

"Just open it."

Elle opened the box. Inside was a necklace with a tiny gold charm in the shape of a Chihuahua dangling from the end.

"It looks just like Underdog!" Elle cried. "I love it!"

"I thought you would," Hunter said.

Elle kissed him. "Thank you so much. You're so sweet!" She snuggled against him.

"When Julia pointed it out to me I instantly thought, 'Elle,'" Hunter said.

Elle sat up a bit. "Julia? Pointed it out to you?"

"We were walking off campus and passed this little gift shop, and she pointed it out and said how cute it was."

Suddenly, the necklace didn't seem quite as wonderful to Elle. But she scolded herself. Why be negative? So Julia had seen it first. Hunter had bought it for her, not Julia, she thought.

"She's got great taste," Hunter said. "I really think you'd like her. You should meet her sometime."

"Yeah," Elle said. "That would be great."

The bell on the door of the diner jingled, and a group of students walked in and sat at the counter. Hunter looked up.

"Hey, speak of the devil," he said. "Here she is!"

Julia left her friends and came over to say hello. She was a pretty girl, just as Chessie had said. Her black hair and red lips reminded Elle of Snow White. And she was tall. Elle felt like a munchkin beside her.

"Hey, you," Julia said, lightly punching Hunter's shoulder. Already Elle could see an easy familiarity between them. *But it's more like brother-sister than lovey-dovey*, she thought. At least, she hoped so.

"Shouldn't you be in the library?" Julia said.

"Shouldn't you?" Hunter said.

"Hey, it's Saturday night," Julia said. "I can't study every weekend, or I'll turn into a pumpkin."

"Julia, this is my girlfriend, Elle."

Julia smiled. "Hi, Elle. I've heard so much about you."

Elle smiled back. So Hunter *had* mentioned her. And he had introduced her as his girlfriend. "I've heard a lot about you, too."

"Chessie says you're the captain of the cheerleading squad," Julia said. "Good for you. She complains that you're bossy, but don't let that bother you. Chessie thinks everybody's too bossy. Nobody can tell that girl what to do!"

"That's for sure." Elle's spirits sank. So Julia had

heard of her from Chessie, not Hunter? And Chessie called her bossy? "She's got lots of spirit, though."

"High school," Julia said. "All the silly little things that seem so important then. And when you get out, you realize it's all just kid stuff. Right, Hunter?"

"College is a whole different ball game," Hunter said.

"Julia, you want to order?" one of the boys at the counter called. "Get over here!"

"I'd better get back to my friends," Julia said. "See you tomorrow night?"

"Tomorrow night?" Hunter said. "What's going on tomorrow night?"

"Professor Albo is having one of her Tea and Talk nights," Julia said. "They're supposed to be fascinating. It's at six."

"Oh, okay," Hunter said. "I'll try to make it."

"Nice to meet you, Elle," Julia said.

"You, too," Elle said. She watched Julia sit down with her friends. They all looked cool and grown-up in their sweaters and jackets. She glanced down at her miniskirt and sandals and felt like a mall rat.

"She's nice, isn't she?" Hunter said. "I'm glad she's my sociology partner. It would be horrible to have to work that closely all semester with some jerk."

Closely? How closely?

"Yeah," Elle said. "She seems really nice."

"Now, back to our regularly scheduled date," Hunter said, turning his attention to her. "Let me put that necklace on you."

Elle twisted around so he could fasten the necklace on her. She fingered the tiny Underdog charm. She did love it, and she was sure it would bring her luck. Anything connected with Underdog always did.

And, she had to admit, Julia *did* seem nice. Elle couldn't think of a single bad thing about her. She wished she could, but she couldn't.

A few days later, Elle went to Pamperella for her weekly appointment. She saw the usual mob across the street at Vernay.

At Pamperella, the doors were wide open. Elle walked in. "Bibi?" she called.

Two burly workmen walked by, carrying a large mirror out of the salon and loading it onto a truck parked outside.

"What's going on?" Elle wondered.

All around her, stylists were packing up their brushes and hair dryers. Elle hurried to Bibi's station.

Bibi was taping shut a box marked TWEEZERS.

"Bibi? What's happening?" Elle asked.

"Oh, Elle, it's terrible." Bibi looked up. There were tears in her eyes. "We're going out of business. The salon is closed until further notice."

Chapter 9

"WHAT?" ELLE CRIED. "I don't believe it! How did this happen so fast?"

She knelt beside Bibi and put her arm around her; they were both crying now.

Pamperella *couldn't* close! Where would Elle go when she had a problem? What would she do without Bibi?

"I guess I'm not good enough to make it in L.A.," Bibi said. "I can't compete with big shots like Valerie Vernay. I might as well crawl on back to Texas and beg some scissor hack in Dallas to give me a chance."

Those words broke Elle's heart. Her beloved Bibi was the best stylist in the whole world!

"You're not going anywhere," Elle said. "You can't leave. I need you. And lots of your other customers need you, too."

"That's too bad," Bibi said. "I have no salon. No place to work."

"You'll get a new position soon," Elle said, "and even better, we'll find a way to reopen Pamperella. There's always room for more than one salon in Beverly Hills."

Bibi brightened a little and wiped away a tear. "Well . . . I guess . . ."

"Just don't leave," Elle said. "Please. Give me a chance to make things better before you give up. Do you promise?"

Bibi nodded. "I promise."

Elle was relieved; she could breathe again. Bibi wasn't leaving! Not yet, anyway. "Will you keep our weekly appointments? You can come to my house, for now."

Bibi smiled. "That would be great," she said. "At least I'll earn a little money to keep me going."

"I'll bet some of your other regulars would love to keep seeing you, too," Elle said. She stood up and started helping Bibi pack. "Don't worry. Before I'm finished with you, you're going to be more famous than Valerie. You're going to be so famous you'll have to hire bodyguards."

Bibi laughed. "You know, I actually believe you. Of all the people I know, Elle, you're the only one who could pull that off."

"Just leave it to me," Elle said—even though she had no idea exactly what she was going to do.

"It's too bad about Bibi," Laurette said. "That Valerie Vernay's career sure took off fast. Look, she's in the paper again today."

Laurette showed Elle a photo on the gossip page of the daily paper. Valerie, an attractive brunette who, surprisingly, looked as if she hadn't done a thing to her hair in years, mugged at a movie premiere with two of her hottie clients.

"I've never seen Bibi so upset," Elle said. "I always think of her as a rock, you know? The person with all the answers. But losing the salon really got to her. It's as if her whole foundation crumbled beneath her."

"So your plan is to make her famous?" Laurette said. "How are you going to do that?"

"I have no idea."

Elle sipped her iced skim chai latte and nibbled on a grape from the fruit-and-cheese plate she'd ordered. It was a nice, warm day, so she and

Laurette had gone to a sidewalk café to relax after school. Elle tried to do her Spanish homework while Laurette read the paper, but the busy street scene on Melrose Avenue was too distracting. So many shiny cars zipping by, so many glossy people in fabulous clothes . . .

Suddenly, there was a commotion down the block. A horde of photographers ran past the café like a herd of cattle, their equipment clanking as they huffed and puffed.

"There she is!" one photographer shouted.

"She's coming out of Fred Segal!" another cried.

Elle peered down the street, but all she could see was a snarl of traffic and a crowd. "What is it?" she asked.

"Let's go look," Laurette said.

They left their table and followed the photographers, who pushed through the screaming crowd, shutters clicking. Elle jumped up to try to catch a glimpse over the heads of the mob, but all she saw was a wall of tall, muscular men and women wearing headsets: bodyguards.

"Who is it?" Laurette asked.

"I can't tell," Elle said. "But whoever it is, people sure are going crazy over them."

The crowd parted, and Elle spotted a flash of

platinum blonde behind the wall of bodyguards. The photographers and the screaming crowd chased after the blonde flash.

"It's Tippi Hanover," Laurette said. "When did she get to be such a big star?"

"The last movie I saw her in was *Little Girl Lost*," Elle said, "a couple of years ago. She was just a kid then, like me."

Tippi Hanover had been a child star for years, but now that she was seventeen and starring in teen movies, her career had exploded. Elle had seen a lot of movie stars in her day, but it had been a while since she had seen one who caused that much hysteria.

Tippi ducked into a waiting SUV as horns honked and people squealed, and then the SUV drove off. A few photographers ran to their own SUVs and took off in hot pursuit. The screaming quieted down to a murmur, and the crowd dispersed. Elle and Laurette returned to their table.

"Well, that was our excitement quotient for the day," Laurette said. She picked up her paper and added, "Look, here's a piece about Tippi. It says that she's in town shooting a new movie called *Rich Girl*."

"Let me see." Elle took the paper and read the

item aloud. *"Yes, that is mega-hot teen sensation Tippi Hanover you're seeing all over town lately. She's on location shooting her latest flick,* Rich Girl. *The adorable star, who went platinum blonde for the role, plays a spoiled Beverly Hills high schooler who gets her comeuppance and learns to love."*

"Aw," Laurette said. "What an original story line."

Elle went on reading. *"The movie costars newcomer Noah Paxton and canine superstar Dexter."* There was a photo of Tippi posing with a handsome boy and a big, shaggy mutt.

"Noah Paxton," Laurette said. "So hot." She licked her finger, touched it to her cheek, and made a hissing sound like water in a sauna.

Elle studied the picture. "That dog is all wrong."

"What do you mean?" Laurette said. "How can a dog be wrong?"

"If Tippi is playing a real Beverly Hills girl, she shouldn't have a dog like Dexter," Elle explained. "He's very cute, but he's too big and sloppy-looking." Elle picked Underdog up and stroked his head. *"This* is what a Beverly Hills dog looks like. Small, neat, fits nicely into a Gucci tote bag."

Underdog leaned hungrily toward the table. Elle gave him a nibble of Camembert cheese, one of his favorite foods. *"And* he likes gourmet food," she added. "Underdog eats French cheese only. No Kraft Singles for him."

"Now that you mention it, you're right," Laurette said. "I can't remember the last time I saw a big shaggy dog like Dexter around here. It's almost as if they're against the law or something."

"They just don't look right," Elle said. "A dog is more than a fashion accessory, obviously. Underdog is one of my best friends. But why get a dog that doesn't go with your lifestyle?"

Elle watched Melrose Avenue return to normal. Tippi had literally stopped traffic. Elle could feel the molecules in her brain pinging around. An idea was coming on.

"Did you see what her hair looked like?" she asked Laurette.

"No," Laurette said. "All I saw was this blinding white-blonde."

"Me, too," Elle said. She looked at the photo in the paper, but in the picture Tippi wore her hair in a ponytail, so it was hard to judge the cut. "I wonder if she needs a new look. You know, to ease the transition from child star to teen queen."

Then it hit her. The brainstorm.

"What if Bibi were Tippi's stylist?" she said, thinking out loud. "If Bibi did Tippi's hair, she'd get more publicity than she could use."

"Sure," Laurette said. "But how do you make it happen? Every blow-dryer in L.A. is dying to do Tippi Hanover."

"She's going to be shooting around town for a while," Elle said. "There must be some way to get to her. If I could just steer her to Bibi, it would rejuvenate the salon. Pamperella would be bigger than Vernay. The press would be all over it. Bibi would be as famous as Valerie. More famous! Pamperella would be the hot salon again. And Bibi's career would be saved!"

"More than saved," Laurette said. "It would go to a new level. Maybe even you wouldn't be able to get an appointment with Bibi if Tippi and her friends attached themselves to her."

"No, Bibi is loyal," Elle said. "I'm not worried about that. I'm more worried about Bibi getting discouraged and leaving town."

"It's a good idea," Laurette said. "There's only one problem, and it's a big one. How do you get to Tippi?"

"I don't know yet," Elle said. "But I know there's a way."

"I think I know someone who can help us," Laurette said. "Let's go to my house."

"Yes!" Elle said. "Margarita. She knows all."

They paid their check and headed to Laurette's house. You couldn't tell by looking at it, but it was the world headquarters of Hollywood gossip.

Chapter 10

"YOU'VE COME TO the right place, girls," Margarita Smythe, Laurette's mother, said. Elle and Laurette sat with her on the living-room couch while she booted up her laptop. Margarita, always a flashy dresser, wore a blue sequined "day dress," feathered mules, and a scarf.

"She has subscriptions to every gossip magazine in the English-speaking world," Laurette said. "And she keeps track of all the Web sites, too."

"Can you give us a little history on Tippi?" Elle asked. "So we can try to understand how her mind works?"

"Yes," Margarita said. "That's very smart. So you can figure out what her next move will be."

"Exactly," Elle said.

"Well, I've put together this short bio for you, *The Life of Tippi Hanover in Words and Pictures*." She opened up a computer file filled with articles and photos of Tippi, beginning with her first job as a diaper model.

"Wow," Elle gasped. "You did all this in the time that it took us to drive from the restaurant? That's amazing!"

"It was fun," Margarita said. "Here, have a look."

Elle opened the files and began reading all about Tippi: born Tinalinda Higbee—the actress's mother changed Tippi's name after divorcing her father and hiring an agent. Tippi's baby face adorned jars of Mushrite Baby Food until she landed her first TV commercial at the age of four. She hawked cereal, grape juice, and peanut butter before landing her first movie role at seven in *Our Eleven Children*. Directors took notice and cast her as the possessed girl in *Haunted Playground*, and as the sole survivor of an alien invasion in *Illegal Aliens*.

Known as a wholesome, sunny blonde, Tippi's image began to change when, at fifteen, she dyed her hair hot pink, traded her overalls for miniskirts, and released her first pop album, *Nobody's Girl*.

That was followed by a starring role as a redhead in the hit teen movie, *The Miniskirt Club*. She had gone platinum for her latest project, *Rich Girl*.

"And the rest is history, as they say," Margarita said.

Elle scanned an article in *Variety* to find the most recent cast-and-crew list. *Costumes: Anna Thorn; Makeup: David DuMaurier* . . . There it was—*Hair: Gianni Cabrini; Miss Hanover's Hair: Valerie Vernay.*

"Rats," Elle said. "Valerie has already gotten to her. She's even on the set."

"Maybe you can change Tippi's mind," Margarita said. "The stars are always changing their favorite stylists, favorite designers . . . They're very fickle."

"It's worth a try," Elle said. "What's the best way to meet a movie star like Tippi?"

"In this case, since she's working here in town, I'd say you should infiltrate the set," Margarita said. "I happen to have the shooting schedule right here."

She pulled up a list from a movie Web site that showed where the production of *Rich Girl* would be shooting and when.

"How did you get that?" Elle asked.

"I have my sources," Margarita said.

Elle read the list. "They'll be shooting on location

in a house in the Hollywood Hills tomorrow afternoon—and Tippi will be there. I guess we'll drive up there after school. What do you say, Laurette?"

"Can we just walk onto the set?" Laurette asked.

Margarita shrugged. "You never know."

"What if we disguised ourselves?" Elle said. "As caterers or something."

"It might work," Margarita said. "Or you could say you're extras, or stand-ins. That's a little more believable, I think. There aren't too many sixteen-year-old caterers around."

Elle and Laurette decided to work the extras angle. It didn't even require costumes. They were Beverly Hills girls already. All they had to do was be themselves.

Elle parked her car along the road leading to the Hollywood Hills house. It was crammed with vehicles, cars, trucks, and trailers. The crew was shooting a scene inside the house, a modern one overlooking the city.

"Do you see Tippi anywhere?" Elle asked.

"No," Laurette said.

They saw the catering truck, which served coffee and snacks. They saw a makeup trailer and tons of wires and lights and cranes and other equipment. Elle saw a man wearing headphones, whom she recognized as Mark Christiansen, the director.

"Tippi must be in the house," Laurette said.

"Let's go."

Elle and Laurette started down the short flagstone path that led to the front door. A large man with biceps the size of Elle's head stopped them.

"Hold it. Where are you going?"

"Um, we're extras," Elle said.

The large man glanced at a clipboard. He fluttered the sheets of paper, looking for something.

"Sorry. No extras today," he said. "There's no call for extras until next week."

"Did we say extras?" Laurette said. "We meant understudies."

The man looked at his clipboard again. "Names?"

Elle glanced at Laurette. Obviously their real names wouldn't be on the list. But they had to try something.

"Uh, Tessie Hanover?" Elle said. "I'm Tippi's sister."

"And I'm Trini Hanover, her other sister," Laurette said.

The man glared at them. "Sorry, this is a

closed set. No members of the public allowed. Go away."

Discouraged, Elle and Laurette walked back to the street. More large-biceped men were everywhere, guarding every side of the house.

"How will we ever get past them?" Elle said.

"I don't know," Laurette said. Then she stared at the door of one of the trailers. "Look—those trailers are dressing rooms. Maybe one of them is Tippi's dressing room."

They walked along the row of trailers, scanning the names taped to the doors. Mrs. Maplethorpe, Mr. Maplethorpe, Scott, Woofie. They were the names of characters in the film.

"That must be Dexter's trailer," Elle said, pointing to the "Woofie" door. "I can't begin to tell you how wrong that name is."

"But none of those other names sound like characters Tippi would play," Laurette said.

"What about this one?" Elle said. She stood in front of a trailer marked LOGAN.

"That *could* be a Beverly Hills girl's name," Laurette said. "Maybe that's her trailer."

"Maybe she's inside there right now," Elle whispered.

She crept up the three aluminum steps that led

to the door and pressed her ear against it.

"Do you hear anything?" Laurette asked.

"Shhh," Elle said. She thought she heard someone bumping around. Then she clearly heard someone say, "But I have to wear false eyelashes. I wore false eyelashes in that Revlon commercial, and now everybody thinks my real lashes are that long. I have to wear false ones for the rest of my life!"

Another voice said, "All right, darling, but that means I must use glue."

There was a clatter. The first voice said, "Get that glue away from me! I hate that stuff!"

"But how do you expect the false eyelashes to stick without it?" said the second voice.

"I don't know. You figure it out!"

"I think she's in there," Elle whispered to Laurette. "Should I knock?"

Laurette nodded. "Go ahead."

Elle was about to tap on the door when it burst open, knocking her to the ground. Tippi bounded out without seeing her, followed by a dark-haired man in tight pants and another one of the musclemen.

"Tippi!" Elle shouted from where she lay, sprawled on the ground. But Tippi rushed by as if she didn't hear. The only person who turned around was the muscleman. He gave Elle a glare so scary she was too afraid to say another word.

"Closed set!" he barked.

Tippi disappeared into the house. Laurette helped Elle to her feet.

"Time for plan B?" Laurette said.

"There is no plan B," Elle said.

"I'm not worried," Laurette said. "You'll think of one."

Chapter 11

"SO YOU TRIED to just walk onto a closed set," Hunter said, "and walk right up to a huge movie star and ask her to change hairdressers?" He laughed. "That's my girl. Bold and fearless."

"It was worth a shot," Elle said.

"Did it work?" Hunter asked.

"Not even close," Elle said.

It was Friday night, date night. Hunter had returned to BHH, his old stomping grounds, to see his old basketball team—and cheerleader Elle—in action. After the game he took her out for pizza at Petronio's. Elle was wearing jeans, a cashmere sweater, and her Underdog necklace.

"You were great out there tonight," Hunter told

her. "The Beverly cheerleaders have never looked so good."

"Thanks," Elle said, basking in his praise. "Everybody was so glad to see you. You were like a conquering hero." The basketball players had swarmed around Hunter after the game. He was a legend at Beverly Hills, and they all wanted to shake his hand.

"The team looked a little rusty," Hunter said. The Killer Bees had lost that night in a squeaker, 65–63.

"It's a young team," Elle said. "Lots of sophomores and juniors. The star player graduated last year. Remember him? The great Hunter Perry? He single-handedly led a losing squad to a championship victory."

"Helped by the greatest assistant manager in the history of the sport," Hunter said, giving Elle a playful pinch.

"Half mushroom, half pepperoni?" The waiter set a hot pizza on their table and left. Elle grabbed a slice of mushroom.

"I'm starving," she said. "I didn't realize it was so late! I'm sorry it took me so long to get out of the gym after the game."

"You were surrounded by your admirers,"

Hunter said. "Who was that guy you were talking to on the way out? In the glasses?"

Elle shrugged. "Glasses? I don't know."

"Kind of curly-haired? Or more shaggy, I guess. Called you Chief?"

"Oh." Elle paused to swallow a bite of pizza. "That was Will. He's in the school senate with me."

Hunter nodded. "Ohhh . . . so *that's* Will."

Elle put down her slice of pizza. "You've heard of him?"

"Not really," Hunter said. "Julia mentioned him."

"Julia? How does she know Will?"

"She doesn't," Hunter said. He refilled his glass from their pitcher of birch beer. "More soda?"

Elle offered her glass for a refill. "I don't get it. If Julia doesn't know Will, why would she talk about him?"

"It's Chessie, I guess," Hunter said. He looked uncomfortable. But Elle could tell something was on his mind. And he was having a hard time getting around to saying it. "She said something to Julia—just in passing—about how you've been spending a lot of time with this guy Will. Campbell—is that his last name?"

Elle straightened up. Something very weird was going on.

"Yes, Will Campbell. I do spend some time with him. I have to. We're in the senate together. I spend time with lots of people. That's the thing about school—there are always other people around."

"Don't get upset, Elle," Hunter said. "I didn't mean to imply anything about you and Will. I was just curious about the guy because he called you Chief. I never heard anyone call you Chief before, and I thought it was cute."

By now Elle was nearing panic mode. Between Pamperella's closing and her insecurity about Julia, her nerves were on edge. "We're just friends, Hunter. We're working on a project together, that's all. Like you and Julia."

"What do you mean, like me and Julia?" Hunter said. "I've told you that she and I are just sociology partners. Are you accusing me of something else?"

"No!" Elle cried. "Not at all. Are you accusing *me* of anything?"

"No, nothing," Hunter said.

"Good," Elle said. "Then there's no problem."

"No problem at all," Hunter said.

But there was a problem, and it hung in the air between them like a curtain. Elle took another slice of pizza, but she couldn't finish it. Hunter sipped his birch beer.

Trying to cut the tension, Elle said, "I trust you, Hunter. I just want you to know that. I totally trust you."

"I trust you, too," Hunter said. He looked her in the eye. She looked back.

"Totally?" she asked.

"Totally," he said.

Elle was glad that that was settled. But was it? The evening had started so well. But now, and for the rest of the night, something felt a little off.

I trust him, and he trusts me, Elle thought after he dropped her off at home that night. *So why doesn't it feel that way?*

"Thanks again for helping out, darling." Eva kissed Elle on the forehead. "I know you're busy. But Zenobia can't seem to shake this flu bug."

"I'm happy to help, Mom." Elle sat behind the reception desk at her mother's art gallery. Underdog curled up at her feet, licking a small piece of Camembert.

Elle had hurried away from cheerleading practice to get there in time, so that Eva could make her past-life-immersion-therapy appointment. It was more important than it sounded. Eva had been told that in a past life she had accidentally caused the great Chicago fire, and if she didn't relive it and forgive herself, she'd be suffering the guilt for all eternity.

Elle watched as Eva grabbed her Hermès bag and put on her large black sunglasses. Her shiny new Val haircut was like a slap in the face to Elle. Elle couldn't believe her own mother could go through with it. But all was fair in love, war, and fashion, she supposed.

"If anyone comes in, you know what to do," Eva said. "Show them everything on the walls, and if they don't like those, show them the prints in the drawers *in order*, from top to bottom. All the best prints are in the top drawers. Got it?"

"Got it," Elle said.

"And I'll be back in a couple of hours if anybody's really serious about buying," Eva said. "That is, if I don't get sucked into some kind of past-life trauma where I can't come out. In which case, check all the hospitals for a woman in a catatonic state."

"Check hospitals. Got it," Elle said.

"Okay, sweetie. Have fun!"

Elle opened a copy of *Us Weekly*. Usually when she worked at Eva's gallery, hardly anyone came in, and she had plenty of time to do her homework or read magazines. It was pleasant to sit in the sunny white room, surrounded by paintings by Eva's latest protégé, and read trash.

Paparazzi shots of Tippi Hanover were splashed across the middle of the magazine. They were the pictures Elle and Laurette had seen being taken on Melrose Avenue.

Elle read the article, all about how fabulously the new movie was going. There was a picture of Tippi in line at the catering truck, waiting for coffee just like any regular crew member. *To prove she isn't spoiled,* Elle thought, though of course the picture didn't prove anything.

Another picture showed Tippi playing Frisbee with Dexter, the dog. *Just like any other normal girl . . . who can't be seen in public without false eyelashes*, Elle thought.

There was a tiny picture of the director, Mark Christiansen, talking to Tippi. Another man, middle-aged and nondescript except for his spiky gray hair, stood nearby. The caption identified him as Stuart Benson, the producer of the film.

Underdog licked Elle's ankle. She reached into her bag and gave him another bit of cheese. "But that's all for now," she told him. "Or you'll ruin your appetite for supper."

He finished his snack and fell asleep on the floor. Elle flipped through the rest of the magazine, reading all about a movie star who was so addicted to Pirate's Booty she'd actually been seen with a powdery white mustache on her lip. Then there was the TV actress who thought no one would recognize her if she wore a coat over her pajamas when she went to the liquor store. Elle loved *Us Weekly*.

The bell over the gallery door jingled, and in walked a prosperous-looking middle-aged man in jeans, an obviously expensive blue shirt, sunglasses, and a baseball cap. Elle went to work.

"Hello," she said, standing up to greet him. "Welcome to the Eva Woods Gallery."

"Are you Ms. Woods?" the man asked.

"Yes, but I'm Elle, not Eva," Elle said, offering her hand. "The owner's daughter."

"Nice to meet you, Elle. I'm Stu." The man shook her hand, then took off his sunglasses.

Huh, Elle said to herself. There was something familiar about him, but Elle wasn't sure what.

"I love the new work your mother is showing now," the man said. "I've had my eye on this red Belova . . ." Elle followed him to the back of the room, where the red painting by Maria Belova hung.

"I love that one, too," Elle said. "Have you ever met the artist? She's so pretty, and she has the cutest Russian accent."

Stu laughed. "I'd love to meet her. In the meantime, though, I've decided to buy her painting."

"Awesome!" Elle said. "You won't regret it. If you have any spot in your house that's kind of lackluster, this painting will brighten it right up." Elle stumbled, wondering if she'd said something wrong, and backtracked. "Uh, not that you'd have anything like a lackluster spot in your house. I'm sure your taste is so impeccable that every molecule of your place is stunning."

Stu laughed again. "Actually, you're right, Elle. There is a room or two that could use a good piece of art like this. You seem to have a good eye. I should have you check my house for all the lackluster spots, and you can advise me on how to brighten them up."

"That's, like, my dream job," Elle said. "That, and designing Barbie clothes, made out of quality fabrics, not that polyester stuff they make her wear."

"I can't stand polyester," Stu said, and Elle knew it was true by the quality of his Egyptian-cotton shirt. "If I had to wear Barbie's clothes, I'd go out of my mind."

Elle grinned. Here was a guy after her own heart.

"My mother will be so excited that you're buying the painting!" Elle said. "There's only one problem. She's not here right now, and I can't handle the sale without her. But she'll be back in a couple of hours, if you don't mind coming back later. After she's had her past life flushed out of her. Or I can have her call you."

"Let me give you my number," Stu said. Elle led him back to the reception desk. He took off his baseball cap and opened his wallet, searching for a business card.

Elle stared at his spiky hair. Why did it look so familiar? Then she glanced at the *Us Weekly* magazine open on the desk in front of her.

Oh, my God, thought Elle.

Stu passed his business card to her. It was all the confirmation she needed. *Stuart Benson, Producer*. The producer of *Rich Girl*!

"What a coincidence!" Elle cried. "I can't believe you walked into the gallery at this moment. It's got to be fate, or some kind of karma or something!"

"Really?" Stu said. "Why do you say that?"

She showed him the magazine, pointing out his picture. "It's you! I was just reading about your new movie. You know, *Rich Girl*!"

Stu nodded. "Yes, we're shooting on location all over town—"

"It's about a rich Beverly Hills girl, right?" Elle said. "Well, I have to tell you, as a BH girl myself, I've already noticed a few details you've got wrong. And I know next to nothing about the movie. So there must be more. The script is probably riddled with mistakes."

"I hope not," Stu said. "But you could be right. What problems have you noticed?"

"Okay, for one thing, the French manicure you have Tippi sporting in the publicity shots. *So* last year. No BH girl would be caught dead in that shade of pink right now. And by the time the movie comes out next year, that manicure is going to scream, 'Iowa.'"

"Interesting," Stu said. "These are the kinds of details I don't know. Maybe I should hire you as a script adviser. After all, you're an expert, right?"

"Exactly," Elle said. "If there's one subject I'm a total expert on, it's Beverly-girl style. I went through a crash course on the subject myself not too long ago."

"What else would you change?"

"Okay, don't take this wrong, because it's a casting problem," Elle said. "But it's crucial."

"I'm ready."

"Fire the dog."

"Dexter? But he's a huge star. Kids love Dexter."

"He's very lovable," Elle said. "But he's *so* not a Beverly Hills dog. At all. No real L.A. rich girl is going to slob around with a big, shaggy, droolly dog like Dexter. For one thing, her expensive clothes would be covered in icky fur—a no-no. For another, he's not very portable. A BH girl needs to take her dog everywhere, like an accessory, like a designer bag. She needs a dog who can go to restaurants, cafés, and clubs. No bouncer would ever let a big dog like Dexter through the door, unless he was a Seeing Eye dog."

"Interesting," Stu said. "I never thought of that. But now that you say it, of course, you're absolutely right."

"Thank you."

"I'm serious, Elle," Stu said. "I really could use you as a script adviser. Would you be willing to try it?"

"I'd love to!" Elle said.

"So what kind of dog *would* a typical Beverly girl have?" he asked.

"I'll show you." Elle reached down and picked up sleepy little Underdog. "Ta-da!"

"A Chihuahua?" Stu said.

"A teacup Chihuahua. Or any other tiny, neat dog. But Underdog really is the prototype."

"Hmmm . . ." Stu studied Underdog's face as if he were an actor auditioning for a part. "Can he act?"

"*Can* he!" Elle said. *Can he?* she wondered. She had no idea. But why not? Underdog could do anything. "Of course he can act." She hoped it was true.

"Great," Stu said. "Why don't you bring Underdog to the set next week and we'll audition him? If he's good, he can replace Dexter."

"Awesome!" Elle had to stop herself from jumping for joy. If Underdog were in the movie, she'd have total access to the set—and Tippi. Plan B was falling into place very nicely.

"You have my number." Stu nodded at the business card on the desk. "Have your mother call me. I'm very anxious to buy that painting."

"She'll be thrilled," Elle said. *But not as thrilled as I am*, she thought.

After Stu left, Elle could hardly contain her excitement. "Underdog," she said, "you're going to be a star!"

Chapter 12

"JUMP!" BIBI SAID, clicking her tongue at Underdog. "Come on, sweetie. Jump!"

"Try using some Camembert cheese. It's his favorite." Elle placed a sticky nub of cheese on Bibi's finger. Bibi held it up so Underdog could see it.

"Okay, try again," Bibi said. "Jump!"

Underdog jumped up and snapped the cheese from Bibi's finger.

"Good dog! Good boy!" Bibi said, petting him.

"See, he's not so hopeless," Elle said.

"He doesn't do much except sit or lie down unless there's cheese involved," Bibi said. "And he shouldn't eat too much of this or he'll get sick to his stomach. It's very rich, *and* high in fat."

Elle sighed. "I know. But it's the only thing he really responds to, trickwise."

Bibi had come to Elle's house to touch up her manicure, but they ended up trying to train Underdog instead. Bibi was almost as excited about Underdog's audition as Elle was.

"Let's see if we can get him to walk on his hind legs," Elle said. She held up Underdog's front paws to make it look as if he were dancing with her. "That's it, boy. Dance!"

She waited until he was balanced on his back legs, then let go. His front paws plopped to the floor.

"I know he can do it," Elle said. "I've seen it a million times."

"He has to be able to do it on cue," Bibi said. "That's the thing."

"Try it again, Undy." She held his paws, but when she let go, Underdog plopped to the floor again. He seemed happy as long as Elle was "dancing" with him, but he didn't want to dance by himself.

"Maybe he won't need to do a lot of fancy tricks," Bibi said. "Maybe all he has to do is look cute. That's sure true for a lot of human actors."

"But he's so smart," Elle said. "I want the director to see that. Maybe some music will help." She switched on the radio and tuned it to a station playing classic disco oldies.

"*Everybody, dance now!*" a disco diva wailed. Elle held Underdog's paws, and he danced on her lap.

"Okay! Now do it on your own!" Elle said, gently releasing his paws. "Everybody, dance now!"

Underdog wobbled along on his hind legs, waving his front paws in the air. He looked adorable.

"He did it!" Bibi cried.

Elle hugged him. "Oh, Underdog, you're the best! Good boy!" She gave him a doggy treat.

"That's a good trick," Bibi said. "You keep practicing that with him. Now let's get him groomed."

Bibi gave him a shampoo. She combed his sleek fur. "He doesn't have much to work with in terms of styling," she said. "Not like a poodle, you know?"

"He loves costumes, though," Elle said. "How about a little plaid bow tie?" She dug through his box of collars, tiny hats, sweaters, and raincoats until she found his bow tie. "He has a teeny tuxedo, too."

Bibi tried the tuxedo top on him and decided on the bow tie. "We'll keep it simple. He's so cute he doesn't need costumes."

"He *is* adorable, isn't he?" Elle said. She picked him up and held him close. "Do you think he has a chance to win the part?"

"How can he lose?" Bibi said. "They're casting a Beverly Hills dog, and he's the real thing. Plus, he dances to disco music. What else does a dog need to do?"

Elle looked at Underdog. Then she looked at Bibi. It couldn't be *that* easy, could it?

"Maybe he needs a few professional lessons," Elle said. "Acting lessons."

"It can't hurt," Bibi said. "I think I know someone who can help. His name is Dag Gunderson. He used to get his mustache trimmed at Pamperella."

"Does he teach dogs tricks?" Elle asked.

"I don't think he'd put it that way," Bibi said.

"How would he put it?" Elle said.

Bibi pinched her nose and said in a snooty voice, "He doesn't teach *tricks*. He teaches *technique*. For true canine thespians only."

"Oh," Elle said. "Sounds very serious."

"He works with all the big stars, that's all I know," Bibi said. "Might be worth a try."

"Welcome to the Barkichevsky Acting Studio for Dogs," said a man with a black mustache and matching beret. "Named for the late, great acting teacher Stanislav Barkichevsky. I'm his former student and worshiper, Dag Gunderson."

Elle and Underdog sat in a circle of other dogs and their owners in a rehearsal room at the Barkichevsky studio.

"Here you will learn the discipline of canine acting in the Barkichevsky Method," said Dag. "Barkichevsky is not an easy path for dog actors to take. But to those of us who believe in the craft—to purists—it is the only path. I applaud you all for your courage."

He clapped. A few of the dogs howled along with him. Underdog looked doubtfully at Elle.

"Don't worry, I'm sure we'll learn something useful here," she whispered to him. "This place is famous. All the dog stars studied here."

"We are privileged to have with us today one of my star pupils, the great Krissy. Here, Krissy."

Krissy, a beautiful, glossy collie, walked into the center of the circle, her nose in the air.

"Hey, remember her?" Elle whispered to Underdog. "We saw her in that movie *Dog Therapy*. About the dog who becomes a marriage counselor?"

"Krissy has just landed the plum role of Buster in *Buster, Part 17*," Dag said. "Which is a tribute to her massive talent, since Buster is not only a male dog but a basset hound. Krissy is such a skilled thespian that she can play another gender *and* another breed entirely."

Elle raised her hand.

"I did not call for questions," Dag said. "However, since you are new to the studio, I'll allow it this one time. What is it?"

"How can Krissy play a basset hound when she's a collie?" Elle asked. "Do they use a costume? Prosthetics?"

Dag grimaced. "An ignorant question. You have so much to learn, my dear. Krissy does not require anything so vulgar as prosthetics. She is able to *suggest* basset houndishness with her masterful *technique*. So that the viewer *feels* he is seeing a basset hound. It's an illusion. Haven't you read the Barkichevsky manual? That is a basic point in chapter one."

"No, sorry," Elle said. "I just got the manual today."

"Well, read it!" Dag barked.

"Yes, sir," Elle said. She found Dag a little scary.

"Krissy will do us the great honor of demonstrating our acting exercises for you," Dag said. "Let us begin with the Dog Actor's Oath. Repeat after me."

Dag placed his hand on his heart and closed his eyes. "I promise to uphold the highest values of artistic integrity in all my work. I will not debase myself with easy double takes and cute expressions. I will not drool or bark without script motivation. No matter how many dog treats I am offered, I will uphold the principles of doggy acting in all my work. *A-ooooo!*"

Dag howled, and all the dogs howled back, sealing their vows.

"Very good. Now, to warm up, let's begin with a simple growling exercise," Dag said. "Anger. Feel the anger. Someone is approaching you. Someone you don't like. Someone you fear. Perhaps another dog, one who stole your favorite bone. Or a child who claimed your squeaky toy for his own. Maybe it's the cruel owner who tied you to a post in the backyard when your favorite TV show was on, causing you to miss it. Feel the anger. Growl, my angels, growl!"

The room filled with low growls from all the dogs, except for Underdog, who decided to keep silent, and a Jack Russell terrier who preferred to bark instead.

"David, Pinky is having a very difficult time mastering anger," Dag said to the terrier's owner. "His work so far is very one-note. It has no depth, no complexity. He jumps, he barks. Have you been working with him at home?"

David, a college guy in a flannel shirt, looked nervous. "We've been working really hard at home, I swear," he said, "but Pinky just isn't a growler. He likes to jump and bark. I can't get him to do much else."

"Well, unless you want to see Pinky's career limited to TV—bit parts and walk-ons in cheap detective dramas, if he's lucky—I suggest you try harder," Dag said. "With his looks, he could go far. But he can't growl? No wonder his career is stalled."

David hung his head. "I know, I know."

"Did you ever stop to think that maybe Pinky just doesn't have it?" Dag asked.

"No!" David said. "No, I know he's got it. Somewhere deep inside him he's a really talented dog. I just have to find that magic button to push—"

Dag lay a hand on David's shoulder. "There is no magic button, David. I keep telling you, *technique* . . ." He sighed as if all the troubles in the world lay on his shoulders. "Let's see how he does with grief."

Dag walked around the room, stopping at Elle and Underdog. "I don't hear growling."

"We're just observing for today," Elle said. "Getting the hang of it."

"A true artist is not afraid to dive right in and work," Dag said. "Remember that."

"I—I will." Elle nodded, mostly so she could look down and not at Dag's piercing, intense eyes.

"All right, geniuses," Dag said. "We covered grief in the last class. Let's see how many of you practiced. Fortunately, we have the virtuosa, Krissy, here to show us how it's done. Krissy? I'll start you off."

Krissy nodded her glossy head. It was amazing. She really did seem to be a kind of diva dog.

"Your master, the little boy you love, has grown up and gone to college. He doesn't live with you anymore. But he was the only one who knew how to play with you, the only one who knew exactly what kind of treats you like, the one who fed you every day, your favorite food, Puppy Chow. His mother puts a bowl of food down for you. It isn't Puppy Chow. It isn't even close. Oh, how you miss little Johnny. The tears spring to your eyes. You remember other sad times, having your biscuits taken away from you, being spanked with a rolled-up newspaper. Being taken from your mother as a puppy. Oh, Mother! Mother! They replace her with a ticking alarm clock wrapped in a blanket and think you won't notice the difference? The shame of it all!"

Krissy lay on the floor, whining. She covered her eyes with her paws. Elle even thought she saw a tear run down Krissy's furry face. Was it possible? She'd never seen a dog cry before, not even in the movies.

"Your heart is breaking," Dag said. "Breaking! Breaking!"

Krissy moaned and howled with sorrow. Then she collapsed on the floor, playing dead.

"Brava! *Bravissima!*" Dag cheered as everyone clapped for Krissy's performance. "And you wonder why she is a superstar. People, you all would do well to emulate this true artist of the stage and screen."

"Someday you'll be like Krissy," Elle said to Underdog. "Rich, famous, and admired by lots of other dogs and—" She glanced around the room. "—Weirdos."

Underdog nudged Elle with his nose. He wanted to get out of there.

"All right," Elle said. "Let's see if we can sneak out. I have a feeling you won't need to show much grief in Tippi's movie."

She gathered her things, picked up Underdog, and tiptoed toward the door while Dag was working with a poodle on her enunciation.

"Your bark must be crisp!" he ordered. "Clear!

No mumbling! Unless you are playing a mumbler. That's a different story." He whirled around and pointed at Elle. "Leaving so soon?"

"Uh, he has to go," Elle lied.

"Geniuses, bladder control is a must!" Dag said. "Do you think Lassie left the set to go? Please! If you leave this room, don't bother coming back."

"Don't worry," Elle muttered as she hurried out the door. "We won't."

Chapter 13

THE AUDITION WAS HELD on the set of *Rich Girl*, since Tippi was busy filming and she wanted to look the dogs over. She wanted to make sure she had chemistry with her costar, whoever it turned out to be.

Stu told Elle to meet him at the Hollywood Hills house where she and Laurette had tried to crash the set.

Elle pulled up, parked, and walked up to the security guard, with Underdog on a plaid leash. This time she was on the security guard's list.

The audition was held in the yard behind the house. Elle was surprised to see all the competition. There must have been at least a dozen dogs there—professional dogs. These were dogs with real acting credits, and lists of credits as long as Elle's forearm.

Uh-oh, she thought, scanning the canine crowd. Somehow word had gotten out that Dexter was toast—and his part up for grabs. Underdog would have to shine, really shine, among this bunch.

But she didn't want to undermine his confidence. Confidence was everything in an audition. So she said, "Look, Underdog! Lots of playmates for you. But not one is as cute or as smart as you are."

Stuart Benson greeted Elle and Underdog with a smile. "Glad you could make it, Elle," he said. "Sorry about all the competition. I was hoping to keep this small, but word got out; you know how it is . . . Anyway, Tippi loved it when I told her what you said about a real Beverly Hills girl's dog. She said you were right, and she wants to watch the auditions herself to make sure we choose the right dog this time. She wasn't a big fan of Dexter's. She thought his nose was too big. I didn't know dogs could have too-big noses, but apparently they can."

"Thanks for giving Underdog a chance to try out," Elle said. "He's got a very small nose."

"I see that," Stu said. "Good luck. I'll be rooting for you—for both of you." He sat down at a long table with Tippi Hanover.

"Can we get this over with?" Tippi said. "These dogs stink!"

Elle checked out Tippi's hair. The color was too harsh for her skin, and the cut . . . well, Elle had to admit the chunky Val was chic. It showed off the long, dangling turquoise earrings Tippi wore. But it wasn't the greatest haircut in the world. Not for Tippi's face shape, anyway. Bibi could do better.

Elle and Underdog waited their turn as Stu called the dogs up one by one.

"First up: Bitsy," Stu called. "Trainer: Dee Schoppert."

Bitsy, a tiny black toy poodle, hopped onto the table. She was a cuddly fur ball and completely adorable. Even the competing trainers said, *"Awww."*

"Oh, my God, I love her!" Tippi squealed. She grabbed Bitsy and held her to her face, nose to nose.

"Ow!" Tippi shouted. "She almost bit my nose off!"

Bitsy's trainer panicked. She grabbed the dog away from Tippi. "That's impossible!" she cried. "Bitsy never bites anyone. She was only going to lick you!"

"I saw teeth!" Tippi said. "Razor-sharp teeth! Teeny, tiny, razor teeth that could have scarred me for life. That just won't do. Next!"

Stu shrugged and said, "Sorry, Dee. Better luck next time. Okay, can we see Fancy Pants, please?"

Fancy Pants was a Pekingese. He couldn't jump up onto the table himself. His trainer had to lift him up. The dog wheezed through his tiny nose and stared at Tippi.

"What does he do?" Tippi asked.

"Do?" the trainer said. "He doesn't do anything. He's a dog."

"Then what good is he?" Tippi said.

The trainer tried to backpedal. "Well, he sits on your lap, and he eats, and he can follow you around. And look—look at his cute little collar! Rhinestones, see?"

Tippi rolled her eyes. "No personality," she said. "Next!"

Dog after dog came and went, but none of them worried Elle too much. Each one had something wrong with it, according to Tippi—too fat, too furry, too smelly, too slobbery, nose too wet or too dry, tongue too rough, tricks too fancy . . . Then Stu called out, "Next up: Napoleon."

Napoleon was another Chihuahua. "Uh-oh, Underdog. This could be trouble," Elle whispered.

Napoleon quickly leaped up on the table and

immediately started a routine of tricks. He did a somersault, he ran in circles, he rolled over, he answered arithmetic questions by barking. He even did a backflip.

"He's adorable!" Tippi cried. "I love Chihuahuas! He's the best! Let's hire this dog."

"There's still one more dog to audition," Stu said. "Underdog. Trainer: Elle Woods."

Tippi waved this away. "We don't need to see any more dogs. This is the one."

No! This couldn't be happening. Would Underdog not even have a chance to try out?

Luckily, Stu was on Elle's side. "We have to give everyone a chance, Tippi. You can sit through one more dog's audition."

Tippi pouted, but she said, "Oh, all right."

Elle led Underdog to the audition table. "Another Chihuahua?" Tippi said. "What does he do?"

"Well, he can dance," Elle said. She turned on a portable radio she'd brought with her. Disco music played. "Come on, Underdog," she coaxed. "Dance!"

"Ugh, I hate disco," Tippi said.

Underdog got onto his hind legs and danced. But Tippi didn't seem very impressed. "Can he do a backflip?"

"No, I'm afraid he can't," Elle admitted. "But

then, not many real Beverly Hills dogs can."

"The script doesn't call for the dog to do a back-flip," Stu said. "Or much of anything, for that matter."

"I don't care," Tippi said. "I think it's cool that Napoleon can do a flip." She leaned toward Napoleon, who stood on the grass with his owner. He looked proud and aloof. Tippi wiggled her fingers at him. "Come here, Napoleon! Here, boy!"

Napoleon could do a lot of tricks, but apparently he couldn't come when he was called. He looked up at his trainer, who said, "Go ahead, boy. Go ahead."

But Napoleon looked back at Tippi and then away, as if he couldn't be less interested.

"Why don't you see what happens when you call Underdog?" Elle said. She had no idea what would happen, but she wasn't ready to give up yet.

"Okay," Tippi said. "Here, Underdog. Here, boy." She held her arms out to him. Underdog looked at Elle, unsure what to do.

"Go ahead, Underdog. Go to Tippi," Elle said.

But he didn't seem to want to. *She must have some kind of inner dog repellent*, Elle thought. Dogs didn't seem to like her much at all.

"They're both losers," Tippi said. "Maybe we should hire the nose-biter after all."

"No—wait," Elle said. She had an idea.

Underdog didn't want to go to Tippi, Elle could tell. He didn't like her much, and Elle couldn't blame him. Still, desperate times called for desperate measures.

She ran up to Tippi and said, "Your earring is caught in your hair. It'll rip right out of your earlobe if you don't fix it first."

"What?" Tippi's hands flew to her long, dangling earrings.

"Let me help you untangle it," Elle said. She secretly reached into her bag and snagged a tiny bit of Camembert. She'd brought the cheese as a treat for Underdog. Pretending to fix the earring, she dabbed the cheese behind Tippi's ear.

"There," Elle said. "All fixed."

"Who are you?" Tippi said. "Did I say you could touch me?"

"Tippi, she was only helping you out," Stu said.

"Try calling Underdog again," Elle said. "He really loves you, Tippi. I can tell."

"Sure he does," Tippi said. "Everybody loves me." She leaned toward the table again. "Come here, boy."

Underdog's nose twitched. He caught a whiff

of the cheese and jumped into Tippi's arms, eagerly licking her face.

Tippi laughed. "He *is* friendly after all, isn't he?" She put Underdog down, but he jumped back into her lap. "Okay, boy. That's enough for now."

Elle took him away. He licked his chops. He'd gotten the cheese. "Good boy," she said.

Tippi looked at Napoleon, who maintained his dignity on the lawn. "I'll show you," Tippi said to him. "You can't snub me. We don't need a dog who does tricks. We need a dog who loves me. I vote for Underdog."

"I second it," Stu said. "Perfect! Underdog is hired." He turned to Elle. "Report to the set first thing Saturday morning."

"Thanks!" Elle said. "You won't regret it!"

Tippi sniffed. "What is that horrible smell? Whatever it is, somebody get rid of it!"

"Right away," a production assistant said. He looked under the table, trying to find the source of the smell. Elle zipped her bag shut and slipped quietly away.

Chapter 14

"HI, ELLE." CHESSIE set down her lunch tray and sat across the table from Elle and Laurette. Laurette was eating a turkey sandwich, and Elle had a salad. Chessie dug into a plate of the cafeteria special of the day, roast beef and mashed potatoes.

"Are you on a diet?" Chessie asked Elle.

"No," Elle said. "I like salad."

"Not that you need to be or anything," Chessie said.

"Are you on a diet, Chessie?" Laurette asked.

"Does it look like I am?" Chessie said. "I burn off so many calories at cheerleading practice I need to keep my strength up. Of course, I'm lucky. I have a good metabolism. Some people can hardly eat a *thing* without getting chub-ola." She looked at Elle and her salad again.

"Elle already ate a plate of mashed potatoes," Laurette said.

"That's cool; whatever," Chessie said. "I didn't mean to imply that she shouldn't. Good for you, Elle. Not getting all caught up in the whole weight frenzy. Very healthy. Just because a girl looks chunky doesn't mean she's overweight."

"Thanks," Elle said.

"Elle is not chunky," Laurette said. "I just want that on the record."

"I didn't say she looked chunky, did I?" Chessie said. "How could you think that? I'd never say something so mean to a friend of mine, whether it's true or not."

"You're a real humanitarian, Chessie," Laurette said sarcastically.

"You really are," Elle said sincerely.

"So, did Hunter tell you? I saw him last Saturday night," Chessie said.

"You did?" Elle said. Hunter hadn't mentioned it. "Where?"

Chessie didn't answer right away. She put a big forkful of mashed potatoes into her mouth, as if she didn't want to say.

"Come on, Chessie, you brought it up," Laurette said, staring suspiciously at her. "You're teasing Elle on purpose."

Chessie swallowed. "I would never do that. I don't kick people when they're down."

"Down?" Elle said. "What are you talking about?"

"Don't get upset," Chessie said. "Remember, you *wanted* me to tell you. You begged me."

"No, she didn't," Laurette said.

"But I will," Elle said. "Just tell me, Chessie."

"Well, he was at Julia's house," Chessie said. "I saw him sitting on the porch with her and her parents, having drinks. Julia was wearing the cutest dress, with a full skirt, one of those neo-fifties numbers . . . She's so pretty. I would kill to look like her—"

"What happened? What did they do?" Elle asked.

"Nothing," Chessie said. "They sat outside talking; then they went inside for dinner. I saw Hunter and Julia leave a few hours later, in his car."

Elle let the news sink in. What did it mean? Hunter had been at Julia's parents' house on Saturday night. He had met her parents. They had all had dinner together. What was that about? Would he have done that if he and Julia were just friends? Or was he meeting her parents because something more serious was going on?

Chessie grabbed Elle's hand. "You poor thing! I can see it on your face. You're heartbroken!"

"Well, I don't know yet," Elle said.

"It doesn't necessarily mean anything," Chessie said. "Sure, most college guys don't visit a girl's parents unless they *really, really* like her. *Really* like her. But maybe he felt like having a home-cooked meal that night, and for some reason he didn't feel like going to his own family's home, even though it's just as close as Julia's, or to your house, which is even closer. It could be anything. There could be dozens of reasons why a guy would go home with a gorgeous girl and meet her parents."

Elle's lower lip trembled. Chessie had seen them. She must know what was really going on. They had probably looked very chummy.

But she trusted Hunter. And he'd said he liked Elle best. He'd said everything was okay.

"I believe Hunter," Elle said, touching her Chihuahua necklace. "I'm sure there's a perfectly logical explanation."

Chessie patted her on the shoulder. "You are so brave, Elle. You're one of the good ones. Some guy will be very lucky to have you by his side one day.

You're like one of those women who marries a murderer who's in prison and keeps insisting her husband is innocent, even though the guy's DNA is all over everything, and there's total proof, and everybody *knows* he did it—"

"You're evil, Chessie," Laurette said. "Stop it. You're upsetting Elle for no good reason."

"I—I'm not upset," Elle said, trying to control herself. If she trusted Hunter, then there was no reason to be upset.

"No good reason?" Chessie said. "I'm not so sure about that . . . Look, Elle, I'm only telling you this as a friend. You should know what's going on, have all the information available and everything. For your own good."

"Thanks, Chessie," Elle said. "I appreciate it. But I'm sure there's nothing to worry about."

"You know what I would do if I were you?" Chessie said.

"Whatever it is, don't do it," Laurette said to Elle.

"Very funny," Chessie said. "It's simple. I'd ask Hunter about it. Just ask him what's going on. I'm sure he'd tell you something that at least sounds good enough to calm your fears."

"Thanks," Elle said. "I will."

*   *   *

"I don't think you should ask him about it," Zosia said. "It might sound as if you asked Chessie to spy on him or something."

Elle had come home from school that afternoon and sat with Zosia while she watched her favorite soap opera. When it was over, Elle had brought up her Hunter problem. Zosia had had a lot of boyfriends and was good with that stuff. Elle preferred not to discuss Hunter with her mother. Eva was so crazy about him she was always on his side.

"But if I don't ask him what's going on, I'll wonder," Elle said. "And he'll hear it in my voice and ask me what's wrong anyway."

"In that case," Zosia said, "you'll say, 'Nothing. Oh, well, there is this boy who keeps asking me out, and no matter how many times I say no, he won't give up. That's bothering me a little.'"

"But that isn't true," Elle said. "That will only upset him."

"Exactly," Zosia said. "He'll start wondering what *you're* up to and be too busy to think about other girls."

"I don't know," Elle said. "That plan seems kind of drastic."

"Promise you'll consider it for plan B," Zosia said.

"Okay. But for plan A, I'm just going to call him

up and ask him what he did on Saturday night."
She reached for the phone. Zosia stopped her.

"At least wait until he calls you first," she said,
"if you insist on going through with this suicide mission. You won't look as desperate."

"Okay," Elle said. "He said he'd call me later
tonight. I'll ask him then."

"Good," Zosia said. "Maybe by then I can talk
you out of it."

But nobody could talk Elle out of it. She knew
Hunter. He played things straight, and he liked people who were straight with him, too. No games.
That would only annoy him.

That was what Elle thought, anyway. Hunter
was her first real boyfriend, so she didn't have
much experience to go on. Just gut instinct.

Elle kept her cell phone by her side all evening,
waiting for his call. When he hadn't called by ten,
she started to worry. She checked her voice mail:
nothing. She checked the house phone to be sure
it was working. It was. What could be keeping him?
He was usually very reliable about calling when he
said he would.

Elle went into the kitchen for a yogurt, trying to
avoid Zosia, who was radiating "Don't do it" vibes
even through solid plaster walls. At last, at almost

eleven, Elle's cell phone rang.

"Sorry it's so late," Hunter said. "Were you sleeping?"

"Not yet," Elle said. "What's up?"

"I was working late at the library, and the time got away from me," Hunter said. "This sociology project is taking up huge chunks of time."

"Was Julia with you?" Elle asked.

"No, not tonight," Hunter said. "She was transcribing our last interview while I looked for new people to interview."

"Interview?" Elle said. The project sounded so complicated and collegey.

"Uh-huh. Last weekend we interviewed Julia's parents."

"At their house?" Elle asked. "On Saturday night?"

"Yeah," Hunter said. "How did you know?"

"Chessie told me. She saw you sitting on Julia's front porch."

"I should have known," Hunter said. "Yes, we interviewed her parents as part of our project. We're trying to prove this theory. . . . Oh, but I'm talking too much. You don't want to hear about this. It's so boring."

"That's not true," Elle said. "I do want to hear about it. What's your theory?"

"Well, the theory is that couples who meet in high school have a low chance of staying together longer than, say, five years. While couples who meet in college or later tend to stay together longer. Even get married."

"That's your theory?" Elle said. "You have to prove that for school?"

"Yeah," Hunter laughed. "Funny, isn't it?"

Elle didn't think it was funny. And she didn't like the sound of the theory. After all, she and Hunter had met in high school, while Hunter and Julia had met in college.

"Whose idea was it?" she asked. "I mean, to do a whole project around that theory?"

"Julia's," Hunter said. "I never would have thought up something like that. I wanted to do high school athletics as a predictor of success in business. But it turns out that's been done. And our professor loved Julia's idea, so we were stuck with it."

"It's a silly theory," Elle said. "Totally wrong."

"Well, we'll see," Hunter said. "Julia's parents met in college, and they've been together for twenty-five years. Her mother told us about her sister, who married her high school boyfriend; they split up before they were twenty."

"That's just one example," Elle said. "It doesn't mean anything."

"That's why we have to interview lots of people," Hunter said. "It's all about statistics. Anyway, enough about that. It didn't bother you when you heard I was at Julia's house, did it?"

"No," Elle lied. "Why should it?"

"Good," Hunter said. "There's no reason for you to be jealous of Julia. I know I've been spending a lot of time with her, but it's just schoolwork. And, well, we are getting to be friends, but that's natural, right?"

"Right," Elle said. "I trust you, Hunter."

"Good. You'd better get to bed now. I'll talk to you again soon. Good night, Buttercup."

"Good night."

Elle hung up and got into bed. She tried to sleep, but she couldn't. High school couples didn't last? She wished Hunter were spending all his time pondering a less threatening question. If he found out that high school loves didn't last, would he dump her? Was their relationship doomed?

Chapter 15

"I DON'T LIKE the sound of that so-called theory," Bibi said. "What made this girl Julia think of that? It's a little too convenient, don't you think?"

She was out by the pool at Elle's house on Friday afternoon, giving her a new haircut. Elle was going to be taking Underdog to the set the next day, and she wanted to look so fabulous that Tippi would have to ask, "Who does your hair?" That was the plan, anyway.

"That's what Zosia says," Elle said, "and Laurette, and Chessie . . ."

"And he's spending so much time trying to answer that question—can high school love last?" Bibi said. "I bet that Julia will make sure the answer is no. And then, Hunter practically *has* to break up with you. It's like handing him a way out of his relationship with you."

"But—I don't think he's looking for a way out," Elle said.

"Not yet," Bibi said. "But by the time that girl gets through with him, he could be. Who knows?"

"Maybe I ought to help him with his project," Elle said. "Find some evidence to boost my side of the case."

"It wouldn't be hard," Bibi said. "I know lots of girls who fell in love in high school and they're still together ten years later. What difference does it make when you met? It's the stupidest school project I ever heard of, don't you think?"

"Definitely," Elle said.

Bibi carefully sawed at Elle's bangs with a razor. Then she hoisted up her blow-dryer and curling brush. When she turned off the blow-dryer, she handed Elle a mirror and said, "What do you think?"

Elle stared at her new haircut. Her plain old straight blonde hair suddenly had a new bounce and shape. There were layers over and under and along her face, and a flattering side part that made it look fresh. It was cool looking, very chic, and not at all little-girlish. It made her look more mature, in a good way—very sophisticated.

"I love it!" Elle said.

"Good," Bibi said. "I'll call it the Elle."

"You're naming it after me? That is so sweet!"

"You're my first guinea pig and model," Bibi said, "and with any luck, you will be the one who spreads the Elle out into the world and makes it popular."

"I just know Tippi is going to collapse in envy when she sees me," Elle said. "She's going to want this cut so badly! It would look great on her."

"The two of you have pretty similar face shapes," Bibi said. "I do think it could transform her career. She's struggling to be taken seriously, to move from child star to grown-up actress. A new haircut could make all the difference."

She took Elle's hand and studied the fresh manicure one more time. "Your nails look perfect," she added. "I love this blood-orange polish on you."

"Tippi is going to die when she sees it," Elle said. "It's the coolest color!"

"She's got to notice it first," Bibi said. "That's your job. Good luck tomorrow." She reached down and picked up Underdog, who was freshly shampooed and groomed as well. "And good luck to you, too, superstar!" she cooed.

"He's going to be great," Elle said, "as long as they don't ask him to do any tricks, and as long as nobody notices the smell of Camembert cheese!"

Elle browsed the Internet aimlessly as she waited that night for Hunter to call. Finally, after eleven, she got an Instant Message.

> Hperry: Elle--u there?
>
> Elliebelly: I'm here. what's up?
>
> Hperry: sorry I couldn't call--still in library. No cells allowed.
>
> Elliebelly: still studying?
>
> Hperry: yes. B-ball practice went late. gd luck tmw. c u tmw nite?
>
> Elliebelly: ok
>
> Hperry: luv u
>
> Elliebelly: me 2

Elle logged off and went to bed. Valentine's Day was coming soon. She hoped things between her and Hunter would feel normal again by then.

Chapter 16

"IS THIS A *skim* half-caf latte?" Tippi screamed. She spat some coffee out onto the grass. "Because I taste milk fat. Milk fat! There is two percent milk in this coffee! Do you want me to blimp up like Layna?"

Layna Malloy, her former costar on the TV show *Funny Girls*, was getting whipped in the tabloids for putting on weight.

"Get me a new latte! And get it right this time!"

Tippi threw her cup at the feet of the production assistant who had brought it to her. Coffee splashed all over the grass and all over the PA's shoes.

Elle, carrying Underdog, had just pulled up to the Hollywood Hills house, where they were shooting that day. She'd gone through security and was on her way to greet Tippi and show off her new haircut when Tippi's temper tantrum stopped her cold. Elle watched the whole thing from across the yard, clutching Underdog nervously.

Tippi was obviously in a bad mood. This was no time to approach her. Elle hoped there was such a thing as a *good* time to talk to Tippi.

Underdog looked at the angry movie star stalking away, still yelling. He looked at the coffee on the grass. Then he looked at Elle. If he could talk, Elle thought, he'd say, *Get me out of here.*

"Now, Underdog," Elle whispered. "I know you're not crazy about Tippi. But for the sake of your new film career, and mostly for Bibi and Kitty, you're going to have to pretend. You can do that, can't you? That's what actors do, pretend. And you're an actor now."

He stared at her, pleading with his big brown eyes. Normally, she'd have spoiled him, given him whatever he wanted. And she could see that what he wanted was to go home and lounge by the pool. But this was bigger than the two of them.

"We've got to help Bibi so she and Kitty can stay here," she said. "You don't want Kitty to move away to Texas. You'd miss her so much! We'd visit her, of course, but it's a long flight, and you know how your ears pop on planes."

She hoped he understood.

"Elle?" A curly-haired young man wearing a head-set approached her, clipboard in hand, walkie-talkie clipped to his belt. "I'm Jim Corelli, AD."

On seeing Elle's blank look he added, "Assistant Director. Basically, I'm the director's slave. Not that Mark abuses his power or anything. Anyway, it's nice to meet you. Is this our new Pookie?"

Pookie was the name of Underdog's character. Elle had convinced Stuart to change it from Woofie.

She held out Underdog's paw for Jim to shake. "This is Underdog. It's nice to meet you."

"We need Underdog in hair and makeup," Jim said. "Come with me."

Elle followed Jim into the house. One room was set up as a salon for hair and makeup. Jim led Elle to a tall, thin man standing beside a tiny chair and surrounded by tiny hair tools.

"This is our dog stylist, Garth," Jim said. "Garth, this is Elle and our new canine sensation, Underdog."

Garth bowed, took Elle's hand, and kissed it. "Charmed." Then he took Underdog's paw and kissed it. "Underdog. What a delight. How gorgeous. You *are* Pookie. I can see it now. You're going to be big. Huge. A supernova!"

He turned to Elle and added, "He's lovely, dear, but the bow tie has *got* to go." He shuddered. "Plaid. Ewww. So Jerry Lewis, 1964. This is the twenty-first century. Get with the program!"

"Oh, sorry." Elle set Underdog down in his makeup chair and took off the bow tie. "I thought it was cute."

"Cute?" Garth said. "This dog is way beyond cute. He's a professional. A star. We have different standards for him now. We don't accept the ordinary. *Cute* is not good enough for Underdog anymore."

"Okay," Elle said. "I'm cool with that."

Underdog's big eyes darted nervously from Garth to Elle and back again. Garth petted him.

"Don't worry, darling," he said to Underdog. "I'll never make you wear anything that's beneath your dignity. You're rising to a new level. You'll see. You'll finally get the respect you deserve. Now—"

He checked a sheet of paper to see what Underdog needed for his first scene. He shouted across the room at a curvy blonde girl. "Candy! Where's that rainbow clown wig Pookie wears in scene five?"

Candy hurried over with the tiny wig. Underdog

tried to jump back into Elle's arms.

"Don't worry," she whispered to him. "Remember, it's all for Bibi and Kitty."

"Ow!" Elle heard a shrill voice shrieking in the next room. "What are you trying to do, pull all my hair out?"

By now she recognized the voice: Tippi.

Elle peeked through the doorway. A messy-haired brunette—Valerie Vernay—struggled to pull a comb through Tippi's strawlike hair.

"If you would just hold still—" Valerie muttered.

"Hold still?" Tippi cried. "I don't have to hold still. I don't have to do anything I don't want to do. Maybe if you didn't put so much hair spray in my hair it wouldn't be so tangled."

"And maybe if you had more manageable hair, I wouldn't need to use so much hair spray," Valerie said.

"Did you just insult my hair?" Tippi jumped out of the barber chair and pointed her finger at Valerie. "Did you? How dare you? How dare you? Mark!" She tore out of the dressing room, yelling for the director.

Valerie sighed and sank into the chair. She looked very tired.

"Elle? Darling." Garth called her back. "Underdog

is squirming. Would you please hold him still?"

"Everybody on the set!" Jim shouted. "Mark is ready for you. Tippi, Underdog! Scene five!"

"Let me just adjust your little red rubber nose—" Garth said, attaching a round ball to Underdog's snout and straightening the rainbow wig. "And—you're all set."

"That's his costume?" Elle said. Underdog looked unhappy. She could tell he didn't like the nose.

"The price of fame, dear," Garth said. "You wouldn't believe the costumes I've seen some stars wear. You know Krissy, the famous dog diva?"

Elle nodded. "We took a doggy acting class with her."

"With Dag?" Garth said. "Isn't he brilliant?"

Elle exchanged a glance with Underdog. "I'd love to hear the story about Krissy," she said, to change the subject.

"Well, she acts all high and mighty now," Garth said. "But when she was a young pup making the rounds of auditions, she'd do anything for a part. I once saw her show up on the set wearing a horse costume. She was trying out for the role of a horse. That's how desperate she was! Can you imagine?"

Elle laughed, pleased to think that the haughty

Krissy had once sunk so low. "Underdog would never do that."

"And that's why I admire him so," Garth said. "Now, take him to the set in his little clown costume."

Jim led them to a room upstairs where they were to shoot the first scene. The bedroom was obviously supposed to be Tippi's—or rather, her character, Logan's—bedroom. It was huge, all white, with a beautiful dressing area and vanity. The floor was strewn with dozens of pairs of designer shoes.

"Put Underdog on the bed," Jim instructed. "Tippi will be here any second. In the meantime, I'll explain what's happening in the scene. Your job, Elle, is to make sure that Underdog does what he's supposed to do."

"What's he supposed to do?"

Jim checked the script. "Um, basically, he's supposed to sit on the bed, dressed like a clown, and watch Tippi while she gets dressed. She's trying to find the perfect outfit for a kid's birthday party. She tries on everything in her closet, but nothing seems right."

"And all Underdog has to do is watch her?" Elle asked.

"That's right," Jim said. "He'll have more challenging scenes later. We thought we'd start with an easy one. He can handle that, right?"

"No problem." Elle put Underdog on the bed. "Just sit there and watch Tippi," she told him.

"Oh, and at the end of the scene, Tippi leans down to kiss him," Jim said, "and Underdog licks her face like he's kissing her back. Okay?"

"Okay."

The director, Mark, came into the room and sat in his chair. The cinematographer took her place behind the camera. "We're ready for Tippi," Mark said. "Where's Tippi?"

"I'm telling you, I'm not wearing this shade of lipstick!" Tippi stumbled into the room, screaming at a makeup girl who was powdering her face. "It's orange! Are you insane? Orange makes me look like a frickin' corpse!"

Tippi was dressed in a silk undershirt and jeans. She faced Mark and said, "Fire this girl. Fire her! Look what she did to my face!"

Mark grimaced. "Your face looks gorgeous, as always, Tippi. Now, can we get to work? We're running late."

Tippi crossed her arms. "Not until you fire the makeup girl."

The makeup girl stood shaking on the sidelines. Elle felt sorry for her. She wondered how many makeup girls Tippi had already run through.

"We don't have time for this now, Tippi," Mark said. "We'll talk about it after we shoot this scene. Positions!"

"Caroline!" Tippi screeched. A woman in a tight skirt and heels skittered onto the set: Tippi's agent, Caroline Aboud.

"What is it, darling?" Caroline said.

"I'm too upset to do this scene!" Tippi cried. "Nobody will listen to me. Nobody cares what I look like. They're trying to ruin my career! Please talk some sense into them!"

Caroline looked at Mark, who dropped his head in his hands in exasperation. "Caroline," he said. "This is an easy scene. Tippi tries on clothes. Her dog watches her. If she could just do that one scene today, everyone's life would be so much easier. We can negotiate the hiring and firing of the rest of the crew once the scene is done. Please convey this to your client."

Caroline looked at Tippi, who had, of course, heard every word.

"Tell him," Tippi said, "that I can't work under these horrible conditions!"

"Tell your client," Mark said, "that if she doesn't get to work this minute, I'm firing *her*. I don't care how hot her career is, I don't care how many teen magazines she's on the cover of, there are a thousand girls out there waiting for a chance to take her place, and if she doesn't go into that room and start trying on clothes when I say, 'Action,' I will give one of those girls the chance of a lifetime."

Caroline looked at Tippi, who uncrossed her arms. "I'm doing this scene under protest," Tippi said. She got into place.

"Everybody ready?" Mark called. *"Action!"*

Tippi scampered around the room, pulling on dresses, skirts, and tops and pulling them off again, trying them with different shoes, and tossing everything to the floor. Finally she settled on a dress and boots. She put her face close to Underdog's and said, "Ready, Pookie?"

Elle motioned to Underdog to lick Tippi's face. He did it, even though he didn't like Tippi, and even though she had no Camembert on her at the time. Elle was very proud of him.

Tippi scooped Underdog up. "Let's go kick some birthday butt."

"Cut!" Mark called. "Excellent. Let's take a break."

"You see," Caroline said to Mark. "That's what

you pay the big bucks for. The girl looks great just trying on clothes."

"Yeah, yeah," Mark said, rubbing the circles under his eyes.

Elle took Underdog from Tippi. She pulled off the clown nose and wig. She knew they must be bothering him.

"You were excellent, Underdog!" Elle said. "Wasn't he great?" she said to Tippi.

"I guess," Tippi said, "but he'd better be good later, in my crying scene. I hope he does good sad eyes."

"He's great at sad eyes," Elle said.

Tippi looked at Elle as if she were seeing her for the first time. "Nice hair," Tippi said. "Did Val do it?"

Perfect! This was just what Elle had been waiting for. She fluffed her hair with her free hand, careful to flash her manicure in Tippi's direction.

"Val?" Elle said. "No way. She's over. I go to this hot new stylist named Bibi Barbosa. She's fantastic!"

Tippi stared at Elle's hand.

"Bibi does nails, too," Elle said, "and makeup. She's a triple threat."

"She is good," Tippi said. "I'm having such a

hard time with my styling team. I feel like they just don't get me. Know what I mean?"

"Totally," Elle said. "That's what I love about Bibi. She *listens*. She's like a shrink! Only better. If only a shrink could make you feel good and look good, right?"

Tippi laughed. "You can't feel good if you don't look good," she said. "If your stylist is terrible, a shrink isn't going to do you any good."

Elle and Tippi laughed over this together. Elle had seen Tippi behave horribly all day. But now she thought Tippi wasn't so bad, if you got through to her girlie side.

Elle reached into her pocket and pulled out Bibi's card. "Why don't you call Bibi? You'll love her."

Tippi shook her head. "I would, but I can't. Valerie Vernay's the hot celebrity stylist. I can't go to someone no one's ever heard of. What will people say?"

"They'll say you're a trailblazer," Elle said.

"It's too risky," Tippi said. "Thanks, anyway."

Now Elle didn't like Tippi as much anymore. How could someone with so much fame and talent and beauty and money be so insecure? Even a trendsetter like Tippi still felt she had to follow the crowd. It was pathetic.

"Oh, well," Elle said to Underdog as she took him back to Garth. "I guess we'll just have to find another way to get through to Tippi. Thanks to you, we've got plenty more chances."

Chapter 17

"ALL RIGHT, Valentine's Day committee," Elle said on Tuesday afternoon. She was talking to just one person, her cochair, Will Campbell. The other member of the committee, Craig Jenkins, was out sick that day.

"The big day is only a week away," Elle said. "I've been kind of busy lately, since, on top of everything else I have to do, my dog is starring in a movie, so I haven't even started working on the decorations. We've got our work *cut out* for us, ha-ha, if you know what I mean."

"That's cool, Chief," Will said. "I'll help. You and I can do a marathon decorations-making session."

"Great," Elle said. "Can you come to my house

tonight? Say, maybe around seven?"

Will checked his notebook. "Sorry—not tonight. I've got a drama club rehearsal. And Monday night's out, too. Same reason."

Elle looked at her own crammed-to-bursting schedule book. "I can't do it tomorrow night—the basketball team has an away game, and I've got to go with the cheerleading squad." Thursday she had a date with Hunter planned, Friday was another basketball game, and the entire weekend was taken up with movie stuff. That left Tuesday, the night before Valentine's Day, which would be too late.

"How about Thursday?" Will asked. "That's really the only night I could do it. I'm going away to my grandmother's house in San Diego this weekend, for her birthday."

"Thursday isn't good," Elle said. She was dying to see Hunter. Their e-mails and phone calls had been strained lately. She really felt she needed to see him in person to reassure herself that everything was okay.

"Why not?" Will said.

"I have a date," Elle said.

"Maybe you could change it?" Will said. "It's the only day that works for both of us. Otherwise, the decorations won't get done. I guess that wouldn't be the end of the world, but . . ."

Elle couldn't stand the thought of the decorations not getting done. First of all, what kind of Valentine's Day would it be without giant paper hearts all over the place? Not very festive. Her big daylong party would be a flop. And it was the first big project she'd planned since being elected president. She didn't want to start out with a failure.

Maybe she'd taken on a little too much responsibility. She hadn't planned on trying to save Pamperella and turning her dog into a movie star—that had just sort of happened. But there was nothing she could do about it now.

"I'm sure your boyfriend will understand," Will said.

"You're right," Elle said. "He should understand." After all, Hunter had canceled on her twice already because he was busy with schoolwork. She had a life, too.

She hated to do it, though. She was so longing to see him. But it had to be done. Maybe he could stop by the set over the weekend to make up for the time they'd have lost together.

"Okay, Thursday night, then," Elle said. "We'll go to my house after school, lock ourselves in my room, and have Bernard bring us dinner. We'll work and work, and we won't stop until we've got enough red, white, and pink decorations to blanket the entire school."

"Sounds awesome, Chief," Will said. "See you then."

"But I made reservations at Sfuzzi," Hunter said. "I was going to surprise you—"

Elle felt terrible. Sfuzzi, the hot new Italian restaurant, had only been open a month, and it was almost impossible to get a table there. She'd have loved to go. And Hunter was so sweet to surprise her—or try to.

"We can go another night," she said. "I'm sorry. I've just got to do these Valentine decorations, and tomorrow is the only night I can do it."

"I understand," Hunter said. "I'm just disappointed. I was looking forward to seeing you. I miss you."

"I miss you, too," Elle said. "So much!"

"What about this weekend?" he said.

"Underdog's got a heavy shooting schedule this weekend," Elle said, "and I have to be there. He doesn't behave well if I'm not with him. He's not crazy about Tippi."

"He's a temperamental guy," Hunter said. "Loves

his Elle, though. I don't blame him."

"I was thinking, though, maybe you could stop by the set this weekend," Elle said, "just to say hi."

"I'll see what I can do," Hunter said. "Call you later. Have fun making decorations. Who's helping you—Laurette?"

Elle swallowed. She hoped her answer would go down smoothly. "Actually, I'm doing it with the Valentine's Day committee."

"Oh? And who's on that with you? Not Chessie, I hope."

"No, not Chessie," Elle said. "Will Campbell."

"That guy Will?" Elle thought she heard a strained sound in Hunter's voice, but it was hard to be sure. "And who else?"

"Well, nobody else," Elle said. "Craig Jenkins is also on the committee, but he's been sick. We're just hoping he'll be well in time to show movies on the big day."

"So, just you and Will," Hunter said. "Okay. Keep those scissor hands busy."

"We will. Bye."

"Bye."

What could she do? She wasn't trying to start anything romantic with Will. They had a project to do together, that was all. It was no different from Hunter's project with Julia. Less intimate, actually. He had no right to be mad or worried about it.

But she understood why he was. Totally. Because she was in the same shoes.

"Ice-cream break." Bernard walked into Elle's room with a tray holding two bowls, two spoons, bananas, strawberries, chocolate sauce, and three kinds of ice cream. Will and Elle put down their scissors and glue, ready for a break.

"Wow," Will said. "First, make-your-own fajitas, and now, make-your-own sundaes. Do you always eat this well around here?"

"Only when Elle is working on a special project," Bernard said, "which is pretty much all the time."

"Bernard takes good care of me," Elle said.

Bernard kicked a crumpled ball of paper aside and set down the tray. "It's a good thing Zosia hasn't been in here. She'd have a heart attack."

"I'll clean it up when we're finished," Elle said. "Don't worry."

Bernard looked over the decorations they'd already finished. Huge cardboard letters covered in red sparkles spelled out the words *HAPPY VALENTINE'S DAY BHH*. There was even a cute black-and-gold-sequined bee with a heart that bounced out of his chest on a coil.

There were cupids shooting silver arrows and lots and lots of hearts of all kinds: glittery gold and silver and red and pink, and even lacy doilies. There was a giant heart covered with smaller chocolate hearts that students could pick off and eat.

"You two have been working hard," Bernard said. "Beverly Hills High will never recover!"

"Look at this," Elle said. She showed Bernard the piece she and Will were working on, an edible mosaic made out of Elle's homemade candy message hearts. "We're using sugar paste so kids can pick off the pieces and eat them."

"But that will spoil the picture," Bernard said. The mosaic showed hearts, flowers, and bees and said LOVE.

"It's made of candy," Will said. "It's not meant to last forever."

"We're going to hang candy necklaces everywhere, too," Elle said. "It will be like going to school in Candyland!"

"And all the kids whose fathers are dentists will be in heaven," Bernard said. There were several dentists' kids in Elle's class alone.

Elle shrugged. "It's one day a year."

Bernard kicked aside more crumpled paper. "Eat your ice cream before it melts. I'll be back later for the bowls."

He left. Elle and Will, in creative moods, made multicolored, multiflavored ice-cream castles and ate them.

"This is going to be the most amazing Valentine's Day ever, Chief," Will said as he licked chocolate off his spoon. "The kids are going to flip! You'll go down in school history as the greatest president on the planet. They should name you queen of the school. Queen for life!"

Elle blushed. "It's fun, that's all. You did most of it. Your ideas are so creative." She loved working with Will. He had a million ideas and endless energy. He was always up for anything.

"We make a great team," he said.

"Yeah, we do," Elle said.

"We should chair the Prom committee next," Will said. "Or, no—what about St. Patrick's Day? That's sooner."

"Green everything!" Elle said. "Green food. Green water in the water fountains!" She flicked her spoon, and a bit of strawberry ice cream flew off and landed just above Will's eye.

"Hey!" He laughed. "You're going to get it!" He

flicked a little chocolate at her.

She ducked. "Missed me!"

"Not this time!"

Elle's cell phone rang. She clicked on just as a bit of banana landed, *splat*, on her nose. She burst out laughing as she said, "Hello?"

"Working hard?" Hunter said.

"We're just taking a break," Elle said, "but we've gotten so much done! I wish you could see the school on Wednesday. You wouldn't recognize it!"

"I've got to get back to the library," Hunter said. "I just wanted to check in and say hi."

"Thanks," Elle said. "Hi." Was he annoyed? she wondered.

"Hi," Hunter said. "Have fun with Will. Talk to you later."

"I'll call you when we're finished," Elle said.

"That's okay," Hunter said. "I'll be in the library, working late. We can talk tomorrow."

"Oh. Okay."

He hung up. Elle wiped the banana off her nose.

"Guess we should get back to work," she said.

Chapter 18

"AND . . . CUT!" Mark called. "Good work, every-body. Underdog, excellent reaction shot."

Mark and the cinematographer began to watch the tape of the scene they'd just shot. Tippi fidgeted while a makeup girl powdered her face.

Elle picked up Underdog and gave him a Camembert reward. It was Saturday afternoon, and the movie crew was shooting inside a fancy Rodeo Drive shop.

In that day's scene, Underdog was supposed to be fussed over by salesgirls while Tippi bought some new clothes. At one point Tippi was sup-posed to try on a funny hat while Underdog looked at her, puzzled. There wasn't much to it.

"You did great, Underdog," Elle said. "You've really got charisma. I think even Dag Gunderson would be impressed. You've got *It*!"

"Let's try the scene one more time," Mark said. "Everybody was great—Do it exactly the same way again."

He stared at the set through his spread fingers, trying to imagine it on film. He frowned.

"Tippi—your hair's a little messy. That needs to be fixed before we go on."

"What?" Tippi cried. "Something's wrong with my hair again?"

"It just got knocked around a bit by that hat you tried on; not a big deal," Mark said.

Tippi looked at herself in a mirror. "I look like a scarecrow! My hair looks terrible!"

Val rushed onto the set with a brush. Tippi glared at her. "What are you trying to do, ruin my career?" Tippi shouted.

"Tippi, calm down," Val said. "Hair moves. It gets messed up. The only way you won't get messy hair is if it's made of metal. Is that what you want? Metal hair?"

"No, I don't want metal hair," Tippi snapped. "What a stupid question. How can you talk to me like that? Don't you realize I could have you fired in about two seconds if I wanted to?"

"But you won't," Valerie said, "because you know I'm the best."

Tippi fumed. "Mark, Valerie keeps talking back to me. It pulls me out of my character. My character is supposed to be spoiled, treated with kid gloves. If someone doesn't treat me that way, I lose my train of thought! How can I act under these conditions?"

"I don't know," Mark said. "Ask your acting teacher."

"I don't take acting lessons," Tippi said. "I'm a professional. I don't need a teacher."

"Then why are you asking me these silly questions?" Mark said.

"Because—ow!" Tippi knocked Valerie's hand away. "You pulled my hair again! Are you trying to make me bald?"

"Tippi, if you'd just stand still—" Valerie said.

"Poor Valerie," Elle whispered to Underdog. "I'm glad Tippi doesn't treat *you* that way. I wouldn't put up with it for a second."

When Tippi's hair was fixed at last they reshot the scene, and Underdog was even better than before.

He could make a career of this, Elle thought.

He had so much personality. But Elle wasn't sure she wanted to spend more time on movie sets. The atmosphere wasn't very healthy—for her, at least. Underdog wasn't bothered by it at all.

"Good work, everybody," Mark said. "Let's break."

Elle went to the catering truck for refreshments. "A cup of water and two cups of green tea, please," she ordered.

She put the water down on the ground for Underdog, who lapped it up thirstily, and took the tea to the hair trailer. Valerie had collapsed in her styling chair. Elle sat down next to her and offered her a cup of tea.

"Thanks," Valerie said, taking the cup.

"Rough day?" Elle asked.

"Unfortunately, this is a normal day for me," Valerie said. "After I'm through here I've got to go back to my salon and handle the huge backlog of appointments I've missed because I'm dealing with the Tipster here."

"I've seen the lines at your salon," Elle said. "You must work twenty-four hours a day."

"Close to it," Valerie said. "I'm getting seriously burned out. But it wouldn't be so bad if Tippi weren't always beating up on me. I don't know how much more I can take."

"It's nothing personal," Elle said. "She's like that with everybody. I've seen her."

"Oh, I know," Valerie said, "but it still hurts. And she's not the only one." She sipped her tea and took a deep breath. "I love styling hair. I really love it. But I never meant to become 'stylist to the stars.' The egos are really getting to me. I want to cut hair, not play nanny to a bunch of overgrown babies."

Elle thought about Bibi. She was a great stylist, too, but she was also a natural therapist, a true people person. She really understood people and knew how to handle them. Valerie was a nice person, but not everybody wanted to be a sounding board for other people's problems. And not everybody should have to be, thought Elle.

"They don't pay me enough for this," Valerie said. "And believe me, they pay me a lot."

Jim Corelli knocked on the trailer door. "Elle, are you in there? We need Underdog back on the set in five."

"Coming," Elle said. "Back to work, Underdog."

Valerie slowly got to her feet. "That's right," she said. "Back to the salt mines. Ugh. How many new ways can Tippi find to call me stupid? Trying to guess is the only thing that keeps me going."

Elle got home in time for a late dinner that night. First she checked her e-mail. There was one from Hunter.

From: hperry
To: elliebelly

Just checking in. Hope you had a good day on the set. Did you finish all your decorations for school? I'll be at the library tonight. Call you later.

Xoxo

h.

Ever since he'd called on Thursday night, when Will was at her house making decorations, Elle had sensed something funny in the tone of Hunter's e-mails—not funny *ha-ha*, but funny *odd*, a tension.

This is terrible, Elle thought. *It's all wrong.* Valentine's Day was just around the corner. They *couldn't* have tension between them. There *had* to be openness and sharing and love. She'd been looking forward to their special Valentine's Day dinner for weeks. She wanted it to be perfect: romantic, not awkward.

But if she didn't see Hunter before then, it might be awkward after all. Elle wished she could make sure everything was okay before the big day.

I know, she thought. *I'll surprise him. I'll go visit him!*

Just to say hi, she thought, and let him know she was thinking of him. To see for herself that things were okay between them, and to let him know she totally trusted him. Then she could plan her Valentine's Day with an easy mind.

"Elle, we're going out tonight," Eva said. She had stopped in the doorway of Elle's room, all dressed up in silk evening pajamas and three long strands of pearls. "It's the Plastic Surgeons' Annual Awards Dinner. Horribly dull, I'm afraid. Anyway, lucky you, you get to miss it. Bernard left some macaroni and cheese warming in the oven for you, with a nice salad. Okay?"

"I'll eat it later." Elle grabbed her jacket, her bag, and her car keys.

"Where are you going?" Eva asked.

"To see Hunter," Elle said. "Just a quick hello."

"Good idea," Eva said. "Don't let him forget about you just because you haven't seen him all week. Those college campuses are full of pretty girls, you know."

"Mom! You're not making me feel any better."

"I'm just kidding . . ." Eva said. "Have fun, darling. Don't wait up. We'll be home late."

Elle drove across town to the UCLA campus; Underdog sat beside her in the front seat, the wind ruffling his fur. Elle realized she wasn't sure where Hunter's dorm room was, but it probably didn't matter. He'd said he'd be at the library, and she knew which one he usually studied in. She'd just have to walk around every floor and search every carrel and lounge until she found him.

She parked the car and walked to the library, Underdog trotting at her heels. She didn't have to look far. Hunter was sitting on the library's front steps. He was facing away from her, but she'd have known that slim, broad-shouldered form anywhere. He was wearing the blue-checked shirt she had given him for Christmas.

As she got closer, she realized someone was sitting next to him. A tall girl. A brunette. They were talking.

It was Julia. She didn't see Elle coming, and neither did Hunter.

Elle got close enough to hear what they were saying. Julia was talking. She said, "So anyway, I don't know if you've got plans Wednesday night, but Kappa's having a Valentine's Day dinner dance, and I was wondering if you'd like to go."

Elle froze. So that was what Julia was up to! Asking Hunter—her boyfriend!—to her sorority's Valentine's Day dance! Did she think he wouldn't have plans? With his *girlfriend*? Whose name was *Elle Woods*, not *Julia*?

"It's semiformal, so you'd have to wear a jacket and tie—" Julia went on.

"Well—" Hunter began. Then, as if he sensed Elle's presence behind him, Hunter turned around. Julia turned, too. Her smile faded when she saw Elle.

Hunter jumped to his feet. "Elle!" he cried. "What are you doing here?"

Elle tried to tell herself to stay calm, not to lose her cool or her temper and say something she might regret. But she didn't take her own advice.

"I just thought I'd surprise you," she said. "I guess I really did surprise you, didn't I?"

"What are you talking about?" Hunter looked angry. Elle hadn't ever seen him look that way at her before. "Were you spying on me?"

"No!" Elle cried. "I'd never do that."

"Then what are you doing here? You haven't answered me yet."

"I just wanted to say hello," Elle said.

Julia stood up. "Maybe I'd better be going. I'll see you later," she said to Hunter. She went inside the library.

"You didn't answer her," Elle said.

"About what?" Hunter said.

"Valentine's Day," Elle said. "Are you going to the dance with her?"

"So you were spying!"

"No, I wasn't! I just happened to overhear . . ."

Hunter stamped his foot. "I don't know about this, Elle. Maybe Julia's right—"

"Right about what?" Elle asked. How could Julia be right about anything?

"About you. And me. Us."

"What did she say?" Elle asked. "I'd like to know what Julia, who's met me exactly once, has to say about me. And you. And us."

"It's nothing. I'd never have taken it seriously, until now. Maybe I should have."

"What did she say?" The suspense was driving Elle crazy.

"She said that you were immature," Hunter said. "Too young for me. Still in high school, while I've grown a lot since I came to college . . ."

"I don't believe this!" Tears welled up in Elle's

eyes. He *was* going to go to the dance with Julia. He was going to blow Elle off on Valentine's Day! And this was his excuse—that she was too young, that *Julia* had said she was too young.

Underdog whined and looked up at Elle with big, sad eyes. Elle picked him up.

"You don't have to say another word," Elle said. "I can see what's going on. Good-bye."

She turned and ran away, as fast as she could. She heard Hunter calling her name. She didn't look back, but she knew he was chasing her. She ran faster, jumped into her car, and drove away before he could stop her.

She had to talk to somebody right away. She pulled up at a stop sign, brushed the tears from her eyes, and speed-dialed Bibi on her cell phone.

"Bibi?" she said when Bibi answered the phone. "How would you like to come over for some macaroni and cheese?"

Chapter 19

"SHHH . . . HONEY, it will be all right." Bibi hugged Elle and rubbed her back. They sat outside by the pool in the warm night air. Elle didn't touch her macaroni, of course. By the time she had gotten home, it had been hard as a brick. Luckily, Bibi had already eaten.

Elle dried her red eyes. She couldn't stop crying. She was a mess. Losing Hunter felt like the end of the world.

"How could he do this to me now?" she wailed. "Right before Valentine's Day? It's ruined. Valentine's Day used to be my favorite holiday, and this was going to be the first one where I actually had a real boyfriend! But now I'm going to hate it forever. For the rest of my life, I'll wear black on Valentine's Day."

"Black! Honey, that's not like you. You'll get over this, you'll see."

"You should have seen what I was planning for our special Valentine's Day dinner," Elle said. "I was going to set up the table over there—" She pointed to a cozy corner near the pool house, under a rose arbor, with a nice backdrop of a starry, moon-lit sky. "A table for two. It smells really nice there, because of the roses. I bought a pink linen table-cloth just for the occasion, and I was going to use Mom's real silver and crystal and china . . . and Bernard was going to make heart-themed foods. Artichoke hearts, and hearts of palm, and heart-shaped pasta with lemon-pepper sauce . . ."

Bibi held Elle while she cried some more. "I know, sweetie, I know," Bibi cooed. "Don't worry. I have a feeling you'll get your Valentine's Day din-ner. Things have a way of working out. You'll see."

"How can they work out?" Elle sobbed. "How can I have dinner with Hunter if he's at that stupid Kappa Kappa Gamma dance with Julia?"

Thinking of Hunter dancing with Julia hurt so much she could hardly stand it. She'd trusted Hunter. But maybe she shouldn't have. Chessie had been right all along. And Julia was right, too. At least, her theory was. High school relationships were not built to last.

"I don't know *how* it will work out," Bibi said. "But I do know that you have a lucky star shining over you, and somehow that star is going to make sure you have a happy Valentine's Day. See the star?" Bibi pointed up into the sky at an especially bright star. It was probably the North Star, but that didn't matter.

Elle blinked through her tears and stared at the star. Was Bibi right? Did she live under a lucky star?

Underdog licked the tears off her face. Bibi gave her another hug. *I* am *lucky*, Elle thought. *No matter what happens. Because I'm not alone.*

Elle had to drag herself out of bed the next morning to get Underdog to the set on time. She felt as if she'd cried all the moisture out of her body; she felt all dried up, like a raisin. She couldn't muster another tear.

But she had to be there for Underdog. And she was happy to do it, because he was always there for her.

"Today's a big day," Elle said to Underdog as she drove to the set. He sat beside her in the front seat. That day the crew was filming at a Beverly Hills mansion not far from Elle's own Brentwood home. "Tippi is probably going to be even harder to handle than usual, but I know you'll be cool and professional as always, Underdog."

Underdog, wearing sunglasses and a scarf, nodded his little head.

"Today's scene is the climax of the movie," Elle said. She'd read the script the day before, to prepare Underdog. "It's the most important scene. Tippi's character, Logan, has finally seen the error of her ways. She has changed from a spoiled brat to a generous, giving, beautiful soul. Too bad that hasn't happened in real life, right?"

If Underdog could chuckle, Elle knew, he would have chuckled appreciatively.

"Anyway, the boy she loves, Chad, played by Noah Paxton—" She paused. Interesting . . . Elle would get to meet Noah Paxton for the first time that day. She wondered if he were as cute in person as he was in the movies.

"So, Chad is picking up Logan for a big dance," Elle continued. "It's kind of a Cinderella thing, with Chad being like the prince and everything, and Logan like Cinderella. She's wearing a beautiful ball gown, and she looks more gorgeous than ever, because now her loving, generous spirit shows on her face. Got it?"

She glanced at Underdog, who clearly got it.

"So, Tippi has to look amazing. And your job is to look up at her in a cute way, with love in your eyes, and also trot along beside her carrying the train of her gown in your mouth. Think you can handle it?"

Underdog looked as if he could handle that with no problem.

"Excellent," Elle said. "As long as Tippi doesn't go completely ballistic, everything should be fine."

She pulled up in front of the mansion. It was surrounded by trailers and equipment trucks and workers with walkie-talkies, as usual. Elle heard a piercing scream come from inside the house.

"Uh-oh," she said to Underdog. "Not a good sign."

The screaming grew louder as Elle walked into the house. She found Garth and deposited Underdog in his styling chair.

"What's going on?" Elle asked.

Garth rolled his eyes. "Her highness's hair—what else?"

"I can't believe you expect me to be seen in public—no, not just in public but blown up on a huge screen and seen by millions of people all over the world—with a pouf on top of my head like this!" Tippi yelled.

Elle peeked into her dressing room. Valerie looked miserable. She had covered her ears.

"I'm supposed to look gorgeous," Tippi shouted. "Not like a refugee from Oompah Loompah Land!"

"But Tippi, you said the last style I tried on you was too flat," Valerie said. "You told me to make it poufier."

"Poufier in a good way!" Tippi said. "Not poufier in a totally hideous, idiotic, stupid way!"

"All right, calm down," Valerie said. "Let's try it again. What if we keep it simple? Just a neat, classic updo." She pushed Tippi down into her chair and combed out the style she'd just finished, preparing to start all over.

But Tippi jumped out of the chair. Her hair was half up, half down, and sticking straight out. She looked like a monster.

"An updo?" Tipi screamed. "A plain old updo? Like I used to wear to ballet class? That is so ordinary! This is a movie. I'm supposed to look *fantastic*! Not like any old girl going to her prom!"

"Tippi, if you would just sit down—" Valerie's left eye twitched. She looked as if she were about to lose it. Tippi was always a handful, but she was worse than ever today. Elle knew that Tippi was being a pain because she was nervous. This was her big scene, and she wanted it to go well. So she took her anxiety out on everyone around her, especially Valerie.

"Why don't you listen to me?" Tippi shrieked. "Anybody could style my hair better than you. *Underdog* could do it better!"

Underdog barked.

"Don't bring him into this," Elle said. "He's good at a lot of things, but don't let him near you with a pair of scissors."

Valerie was shaking. Her left eye was twitching like crazy now.

Uh-oh, Elle thought. *This is it. She's going to crack.*

"You'd rather have a dog do your hair?" Valerie said quietly. "Fine. Underdog can do your hair. I'm sure not going to."

Tippi stared at her openmouthed as Valerie grabbed a few of her things. "Good luck with your big scene today," Valerie said. "By the way, your hair looks like crap."

She stalked out of the room. Tippi's hands flew to her hair. She turned to look in the mirror and screamed at the sight of herself. Then she ran after Valerie.

"Wait! You can't leave me like this!" Tippi shouted. "I'll ruin you forever! You'll never work in this town again! Your career is over, Valerie. Do you hear me? Over!"

Valerie didn't stop. She didn't look back. She was gone. And Tippi was left half dressed in her costume, her hair like a fright wig. She started to cry. "What am I going to do now?"

Mark, the director, came into the dressing room. "What is going on around here?" he demanded. "Why did Valerie just tell me she quit? On the most important day of shooting? When we're already a month behind schedule?"

"It's not my fault," Tippi said. "Look what she did to me!"

Elle knew Mark didn't care who had done what to whose hair. He just wanted to get to work. She saw her big chance and she took it.

"I know a great hairstylist who can be on the set in five minutes," Elle said.

"Is she a lion tamer, too?" Mark asked, glancing at Tippi.

"She's great with people," Elle said. "Give her a try."

175

"What choice do I have?" Mark said. "Call her, Elle. And Tippi—" He shook his finger at her threateningly. "You'd better not drive this stylist away. I want this scene finished today. If not, I'll tell every director I know how difficult you are. And you don't want to be known as difficult. You can get away with it for a while, but eventually it comes back to bite you in the butt."

Tippi dried her eyes. "Your stylist better be good, Elle," she said.

"She is," Elle said, getting out her cell phone.

"Makeup!" Tippi screeched. "Somebody, come fix my face!"

Elle speed-dialed Bibi. "Bibi? I'm on the movie set. We need you. Get over here, right now!"

Chapter 20

"WHEN WE HAVE TIME, I'm going to add a few low-lights to your hair," Bibi said to Tippi in her soothing Texas twang. "Your color's getting a little flat. It's not as flattering as it could be."

"You're so right," Tippi said. "I knew something was wrong, but I couldn't put my finger on it."

Elle sat and watched as Bibi combed out Tippi's hair. Her plan: to transform Tippi from prettier-than-average starlet to fabulous force of nature.

Bibi hadn't been able to do much with the raging monster Tippi was when she arrived. So, first, she had calmed Tippi down. She'd reassured Mark that they'd start shooting soon, only a little late, but that he should leave Tippi to her and not interfere.

Then, with Elle and Underdog as assistants, Bibi went into Tippi's dressing room and closed the door. She put on some soft music and, without letting Tippi realize exactly what she was doing, gently rubbed Tippi's head. She talked to Tippi and listened to her endless litany of complaints. Underdog even let Tippi hold him while they worked, after a little coaxing.

"To me, the way to go for this scene is to highlight your face," Bibi said to Tippi. "You've got a beautiful face. One of the great movie faces of all time."

Tippi beamed. Elle kept herself from rolling her eyes. Bibi was buttering Tippi up, and it worked only too well. At the same time, what Bibi said was true. Tippi was a star for a reason. She had a great movie face.

"So, I'm going to create a new haircut, just for you," Bibi said, "but I have to warn you—it's a little shorter than you've ever gone before. You'll see lots of hair on the floor. Don't get scared. Do I have your permission?"

Tippi looked at Bibi's face in the mirror. She bit her lip. Bibi played with Tippi's hair, showing her how a shorter cut might look.

"Especially if we temper the blonde with a little

red," Bibi said. "You'll look fabulous, and different from anyone else in Hollywood."

"But not *too* different, right?" Tippi said. "I don't want to look like a freak."

"Never," Bibi said. "Just different enough."

Tippi eyed her reflection in the mirror.

"A movie star shouldn't look like everybody else," Bibi said. "A movie star should stand out from the crowd."

"Go for it," Tippi said.

Bibi started cutting. To distract Tippi from what was happening, she turned her chair away from the mirror. Elle recognized the technique as a Bibi specialty: her way of taking the client's mind off her problems.

"Do you want to practice some of your lines with me and Elle?" Bibi asked Tippi. "I bet Underdog could use the rehearsal."

Elle laughed. "He sure could. He doesn't have many lines, though. Mostly *Ruff! Ruff ruff!* And *Grrr . . .*"

Tippi laughed and petted Underdog. He licked her fingers. Elle knew how good it must have felt to Tippi to have his warm, furry little body on her lap. Just being near him could make one's troubles melt away. . . .

"Good dog," Tippi said. "What a good dog . . ."

"Here." Elle took a bit of cheese out of her bag. "If you want to give him a real treat, try some of this Camembert."

Tippi wrinkled her nose. "Dogs don't eat cheese."

Elle shrugged. "He loves it."

Tippi took the cheese and gave it to Underdog, who lapped it up. "You're right!" Tippi said.

All the while, Bibi was cutting and shaping and styling her hair. It worked wonders soothing Tippi's nerves. Somehow Bibi had managed to get Tippi to stop throwing tantrums and act like a human being. She was a great starlet-wrangler.

"What do you think about my nails?" Tippi asked Bibi. "I'm so sick of French manicures. But nothing else looks as good."

"We'll try something new on you after your hair's done," Bibi said. "I just discovered a new look—the Estonian manicure, brought over by all those Eastern European models. Wait until you see it."

Bibi finished cutting. She rubbed in some styling gel and started blow-drying. By the time she was done, Tippi was so calm she was practically meditating. Underdog was asleep in her lap. She woke him, and he jumped into Elle's arms.

Bibi blew on the end of her dryer as if it were a smoking gun. Elle looked up at Tippi and gasped. She was beautiful, completely transformed. Her hair was shorter and layered, with bangs. It complemented her face in a new way, bringing out her big eyes and her cheekbones. She didn't look like a cookie-cutter teen star anymore. She looked like a full-blown grown-up movie superstar.

"Oh, my God," Elle said.

"What? What?" Tippi cried, her nerves coming back to her. "Is it bad? Is it awful?"

"See for yourself." Bibi turned her toward the mirror.

Tippi stared at herself in shock. Elle braced herself for another tantrum. What if the change was too much for Tippi?

Tippi screamed. Bibi and Elle exchanged glances. Had they failed?

"I love it!" Tippi squealed. *"You're a genius!"*

"I call it the Tippi," Bibi said.

"You look fantastic," Elle said.

Jim appeared, his walkie-talkie crackling. "Is Tippi ready yet? We need her on the set."

"Wait," Elle said, getting out her camera phone. "Let's get a picture of the Tippi on the day it was born."

She aimed her phone at Tippi and took a picture. The flash went off. Elle studied the shot.

"That's good," she said. "Now one of you and Bibi together."

Tippi posed with her arm around Bibi. The flash went off again. "Just a couple more . . ." Elle said. She wanted to get the perfect shot—a shot no gossip column would be able to resist.

"I'll take one of the three of you together," Jim said. Elle posed with Underdog, Tippi, and Bibi.

"Awesome," Jim said. "Okay, enough pictures. Tippi, get dressed."

"Where's my costume?" Tippi said. A dresser came in to help her.

"Your hair looks amazing," the dresser said.

"Thanks," Tippi said. "Ow! Be careful! That zipper pinched me!"

"I'm sorry," the dresser said.

Elle e-mailed the photos to herself. She'd send them off to all the papers as soon as she got home.

"Watch it!" Tippi snapped at the dresser. "Are you an idiot? You totally pinched me!"

Elle sighed. Some things never changed.

"And—Action!"

Tippi appeared at the top of a long, winding

staircase, dressed in her ball gown, her new hairdo topped by a tiara. Noah Paxton, as Chad, stood in a tuxedo at the bottom of the staircase, waiting for his princess to descend. Underdog trotted behind Tippi, wearing a little red velvet vest and carrying her train in his tiny teeth. He was very good at not getting too much dog drool on the dress. Elle was proud of him.

But she felt a little sad, watching Tippi float into Noah's arms (and he was *cuter* in person than in the movies), glowing for her fairy-tale happy ending. Elle missed Hunter. She thought about Valentine's Day, only three days away, and felt a pang. If only she could have a fairy-tale happy ending, too.

"Cut!" Mark called. "Great job, everybody. Tippi, you look fantastic. Better than I've ever seen you."

Tippi beamed. "Thank you!"

Mark turned to Elle. "Who did you bring in to do her hair?"

"She's right here." Elle grabbed Bibi's wrist. Bibi smiled under her cowboy hat. "Her name is Bibi Barbosa, and she's a genius. Tippi said so herself."

"Nice to meet you, Bibi," Mark said. "I hope you're free for the next few weeks, because we need you here. You're hired."

When he turned away, Elle and Bibi jumped up and down for joy, trying to keep excited squeals from bursting out of their mouths.

"You did it!" Elle said.

"No, Elle—*we* did it," Bibi said.

Chapter 21

"EXCUSE ME. Coming through. Oops—excuse me." Elle and Underdog fought through the crowds and the furniture movers at Pamperella the next afternoon, looking for Bibi. Elle had broken a nail and needed to fix it. Even though her Valentine's Day date was canceled, she still had the school party to think of. And she didn't want to be seen with a chipped nail, no matter what.

"Bibi! There you are!"

Bibi was surrounded by eager clients, reporters, photographers, and a film crew from Style TV. The movers were installing new equipment and fantastic new furniture. Bibi waved to Elle, but Elle couldn't even get close.

"Wow," Elle said to Underdog. "I knew she'd get big after inventing the Tippi, but I didn't think it would happen so fast."

Elle had made sure the tabloids had the photo of Bibi with Tippi showing off her new haircut by the end of the previous day. That morning, it was in all the papers. Just like that!

Pamperella had reopened and was swamped with customers. The salon was saved. Bibi's career was taking off for the stratosphere. She wasn't moving back to Texas. She wasn't going anywhere. She was the new stylist to the stars! And Elle was thrilled for her.

Bibi broke away from the pack and ran to hug Elle. "Can you believe this? It's crazy! But it's like a dream."

"You deserve it," Elle said.

Bibi picked up Elle's hand and frowned at the broken nail. "Let's get that fixed right away. No matter how busy I get, I'll always have time for my favorite customer."

Bibi led her to a quiet back room and fixed her nail. "Tippi's been talking me up to everybody," Bibi said. "I've gotten calls from all these movie stars, begging me for appointments! It's wild!"

She filed Elle's nail and smiled at Underdog. "I

was so busy yesterday I almost forgot to say how proud I was of Underdog. My little actor! I told Kitty all about it, and I could tell she was very proud, too. You're going to be a big star soon, Underdog."

Elle patted him. "I don't know. If he really wants to keep up with this acting thing, I'll go along with it. But if he's willing to retire after this movie, I'll be relieved. The movie business is a crazy world."

"It sure is," Bibi said. "And I love it!"

With nails freshly done, Elle left the zoo that was Pamperella. She peered across the street at Vernay, which only a week earlier had been as busy as Pamperella was now.

Elle crossed the street and went inside Vernay. A few women sat in the lounge waiting for their appointments, but nothing like the crowds that had been there before. Pamperella was the hot new salon now.

Valerie stood behind a partition, blow-drying a young woman's hair. She smiled when Elle and Underdog walked in.

"Hi, Elle," she said. "How's life in the torture chamber they call Tippi Hanover's dressing room?"

Elle laughed. "Same as always, pretty much. She'll never be voted Humanitarian of the Year, but she was your biggest client. I hope you don't mind losing her."

"I'm just glad to be out of there," Valerie said. "I couldn't handle Tippi anymore, or any of those other bratty starlets. I've still got a thriving business, and good, pleasant customers like Daisy here."

Daisy, who did seem to be a nice person, looked up and smiled at the sound of her name.

"I'm happy for Bibi," Valerie said. "She's good— very good. There's plenty of room in Beverly Hills for two hot salons. There are certainly enough beauty-obsessed people in this town."

"That's for sure," Elle said.

"And if Bibi takes some business off my hands, that's okay with me," Valerie said. "It leaves me more time to have a life. I hope Bibi won't let the stress get to her the way it got to me."

"I think she'll be okay," Elle said.

Things had worked out well for Valerie and Bibi. Elle was glad. The only thing that hadn't worked out was her own life—and Hunter. She hadn't spoken to him since their fight on Saturday night.

"Call him," Laurette said. She and Elle were

lounging by the pool later that afternoon. "Come on. You know you want to. You're dying to."

"Of course, I'm dying to," Elle said. She missed him so much she felt as though her rib cage might crack in two from the pain. "But I can't call him. I just can't. How could he think I'd spy on him?"

"If you call him you can explain that you weren't spying," Laurette said. "Maybe once he understands—"

"It doesn't matter," Elle said. "He's going to that sorority dance with Julia anyway. It's over."

"You don't know that for sure," Laurette said. "Maybe if you call him he won't go."

"I don't want him not to go because I called him," Elle said. "I want him not to go because he doesn't want to go, because he doesn't want to be with anyone but me."

"But what if he ends up going with Julia just because he thinks you don't want to see him?" Laurette said. "One of you has to give in sometime, or you'll never speak to each other again."

The thought of never speaking to Hunter again hurt like a punch in the stomach. But Elle was proud. She wouldn't humiliate herself. If he liked another girl better, she'd just have to learn to live with it, somehow, after crying her eyes out first.

But there was also another reason not to call.

"I'm afraid of what I might find out," she admitted to Laurette. "What if he says, 'It's over. I'm with Julia now'? I can't bear to hear him say those words, even if they're true."

"I'd bet anything they're not true," Laurette said. "Anyway, if he dumps you for Julia, you can always spend Valentine's Day with Will Campbell. I'm sure he'd be happy to spend it with you."

"Will's nice," Elle said, "but he's not Hunter."

Chapter 22

MONDAY PASSED, and Monday night, and there was still no call from Hunter. Elle carried her boxes of Valentine's Day supplies to school on Tuesday morning with a heavy heart.

"Elle!" Chessie said. "I saw your picture in the paper yesterday, with that hairdresser you hang with? And Tippi Hanover. She's so pretty. You looked okay, too! I mean, considering you were standing next to one of the most gorgeous girls on the face of the earth, you didn't look too bad. If anyone even notices that you're in the picture. But don't worry, they probably won't. I mean, if you're looking at a picture of Tippi and she's not standing next to a hottie like Noah Paxton, who cares who she's with? Right?"

"It's true," Elle said. "Bibi made her look fantastic."

"Bibi?" Chessie said. "I think the genes Tippi was born with had *something* to do with it."

"Of course," Elle said. "I didn't mean—"

She was too tired to get into a whole circular-logic thing with Chessie.

Luckily, Laurette stepped in. She strong-armed Chessie like a bodyguard or a secret-service agent, blocking her so that Elle could get through the hall to her locker undisturbed.

"Keep your distance, please, Chessie," Laurette said. "President Elle coming through. Official business."

That wasn't enough to stop Chessie. Not even close. "So what are you doing for Valentine's Day, Elle?" she asked.

"Um—I'm not sure," Elle said.

"It's tomorrow, you know," Chessie said.

"I know," Elle said.

"That means you don't have time to fool around," Chessie said. "I'm so excited! I'm expecting a *lot* of valentines. I'm setting up a special mail basket on my locker, just to hold them all."

"But there's one problem. You don't have a

boyfriend," Laurette said, "do you?"

"Not technically," Chessie said, "but I happen to know a whole lot of boys are too shy to tell me how much they like me. Especially Chris Rodriguez."

Chris Rodriguez, Homecoming King and senior hottie, was the object of affection of many eager girls. He wasn't shy.

"I'm hoping tomorrow he'll work up the courage to let me know how he really feels," Chessie said. "You'd think he could at least manage an anonymous note. So, Elle, you never said what you're going to do. Sit at home alone and listen to sad music?"

"She's going to be with Hunter, of course," Laurette said.

"Really?" Chessie said. "That's not what I heard. . . ."

"What did you hear?" Elle asked.

Chessie looked her in the eye. "Oh, Elle. No! It's really true, isn't it? I didn't want to believe it, but—"

"What's really true?" Laurette said.

"You . . . and Hunter . . ." Chessie made a slicing motion across her throat.

"It isn't true," Laurette said. "Elle just hasn't talked to him in a couple of days, which is completely normal."

"Normal?" Chessie said. "Did you have a fight?"

"Why don't *you* tell *us?*" Laurette said. "You seem to know everything."

Chessie ignored her. "Elle, you poor thing. But I have to say I saw it coming. You did, too, didn't you?"

Elle swallowed hard, trying to keep from crying. Was Chessie right? Had she and Hunter broken up for real? Should she have seen it coming long ago? Hearing Chessie talk about Hunter that way made it all seem worse than ever.

"You must feel terrible," Chessie said. "Just *awful.* If I were you, I couldn't even show my face at school. I'd probably lock myself in my room and not come out for a year—no, two years. I'd probably sit in front of the TV and eat Pirate's Booty and Devil Dogs until I weighed about five hundred pounds and had zits all over my face. And then I'd *really* not want to show my face, so I guess I'd join a convent or something. Maybe the rigors of religious life would help me slim down a bit. Then, by the time I'm fifty or sixty, I could finally come out into the world, a plain, simple spinster, not attractive—ugly, even—but spiritually good and pure at heart. If I were you, I mean."

Elle was close to tears, even though she wasn't

quite sure what Chessie was talking about.

"What are you raving about now, Chessie?" Laurette said. She turned to Elle and protectively pulled her away by the arm. "Let's get out of here before she starts predicting *my* future."

Will scooted up to them. "Glad you're here, Chief. Are we on to hit this place with a love bomb after school today?"

Just the sight of him—in place of Chessie—cheered Elle up a lot. "We're on," Elle said, "after cheerleading practice. Say, four thirty?"

"It's a date," Will said. The first bell rang. "Ugh, Calculus. See you later, Chief." He hurried away.

Elle put away the decorations and got out her books. "Will you help us, too, Laurette?" Elle asked.

"No problem," Laurette said.

"Why do you want her there?" Chessie said. "Didn't you hear what Will said? It's a date. You don't want Laurette around on a date."

"It's not a date," Elle said. "He didn't mean it that way."

"How do you know?" Chessie said. "He's the perfect rebound guy, to help you get over Hunter, and your excruciating heartbreak."

"Elle's not heartbroken," Laurette said, "because nothing bad has happened. Usually you need something bad to happen before you can be heart-broken."

"Brave girl," Chessie said, "trying to pretend nothing's wrong. I'll play along, if it makes you feel better. I'll come by and help decorate, too."

"The more the merrier," Elle said.

"Not in this case," Laurette said.

Chapter 23

"ELLE, YOU HAVEN'T written a new cheer in a while," Chloe said at cheerleading practice that afternoon. "I think the crowd is getting tired of all our old routines."

"Well—" Elle actually had written several new cheers recently. The problem was, they weren't very cheerful. So she hesitated to share them. "I have written some. I don't know if you'll like them."

"Try us," P.J. said.

"Here goes," Elle said. She gathered up her pom-poms.

> *Hey! Ungawa! Who's got the power? I*
> *don't know, but it isn't me, feeling sad as*

*I can be. B-ball boys who shoot and
score, don't forget who it's all for.
Remember when you make that play,
tomorrow is St. Valentine's Day. Be nice
to all the girls and boys. Don't treat them
like old cast-off toys. Go, Bees!*

The other girls stared at her blankly.

"Don't like that one, huh?" Elle said. "Here's another."

*The Venice Vultures think they're so
smart? Stomp them like you stomped
my heart! Have no mercy, have no fear,
shout it out like Paul Revere: "Valentine's
Day is coming! Valentine's Day is coming! The saddest day of all the year."*

More blank looks. At last Chessie spoke. "Elle, have you seen a doctor lately?"

"Those are the most cheerless cheers I ever heard," Chloe said.

"I know," Elle said, "but that's what's been on my mind lately. I cheer the way I feel. Usually I feel great, but the past few days have been rough. I express my feelings through cheering, good or bad."

"Have you ever thought of writing poetry instead?" P.J. asked. "Or maybe depressing song lyrics?"

"What about you guys?" Elle asked. "Have any of you come up with a new cheer lately?"

"I'm glad you asked," Chessie said. "Here's one I've been working on."

> *The boy you like does not like you. Here*
> *is what you've got to do: S-E-T-T-L-E.*
> *Settle! That's right, settle! Settle for a*
> *lesser boy. That's the best that you can*
> *do. Not me, of course—I can do better.*
> *I'll get the boy who's dumping you!*

"We're not chanting *that*," Chloe said.

"That has even less to do with sports than Elle's cheers," P.J. said.

"So? You think you can do better?" Chessie said.

"Maybe," P.J. said.

> *B-E-V-E-R-L-Y!*
> *Jump so high you reach the sky! Go,*
> *Bees! Don't you let us down; we'll kick*
> *the losers out of town. While we're at it,*
> *here's a shout to Craig, a jerk, there is no*

doubt. Forget my birthday? Do you dare?
Replace me with a girl named Claire? I'll
cut up all your underwear and kick
your butt to Delaware.

"What do you think?" P.J. asked.

"It started off okay," Chloe said. "Then it went kind of downhill."

"Boy, this squad has got heavy-duty boy trouble," Elle said. "We need something to cheer us up, fast."

"Let's cancel Valentine's Day," P.J. said.

"We can't do that," Elle said. "Everyone's looking forward to it."

"I'm not," P.J. said.

"I'm not, either," Chloe said.

"I am," Chessie said. "Losers."

"We're not losers," Elle said. "And you know what? We'll show everyone in school that we're not. We'll have the best Valentine's Day ever, broken hearts or not. Are you with me?"

No one answered.

"There's going to be a lot of good food," Elle said coaxingly.

"Well—" P.J. said.

"And lots of fun all day long," Elle said, "with

very little schoolwork getting done . . ."

"Hmmm . . ." Chloe said. "At least it will be better than a regular school day."

"Way better!" Elle said. "There will even be love potion, as a last resort. Bowls and bowls of it. We'll have a great time! Are you with me?"

"Yeah!" the cheerleaders shouted.

"I can't hear you!" Elle taunted.

"Yeah! Valentine's Day!"

"All right." Elle was pleased. She and her sisters in misery were going to laugh in the face of Valentine's Day loneliness—or try to, anyway.

"That love potion had better be good," Chessie said.

The halls buzzed with activity after classes that afternoon. Most of the student senate had volunteered to help decorate, under Elle's and Will's leadership.

"Where do you want the disco ball, Chief?" Will asked. He held out a large, mirrored ball.

"In the front entrance, hanging from the middle of the ceiling," Elle said. She planned to have an all-day dance party in the large front lobby of the school. As soon as the students walked through the doors, the dancing would begin. And if they had a free period, or lunch, or if a sympathetic teacher let them out of class, they could go back to the lobby and dance some more.

"Let's set this long table here, to the side," she said to Laurette. The two of them carried an extra-long cafeteria table and pushed it against one wall of the lobby. Elle draped a red tablecloth over it. Laurette pinned a sign on the wall just above that said: LOVE POTION.

"What's in the love potion?" Chessie asked. "Nothing illegal, I hope."

"Zosia's secret recipe," Elle said. "She says if you take a sip while looking at the one you love, he'll love you back. There's a special herb in it."

"Mostly juices, though, right?" Chessie said.

"Red ones," Elle said. "The secret ingredient is mint."

By dinnertime the school looked beautiful. The halls glittered and sparkled magically with red and gold and silver.

Everyone else had gone home. Elle and Laurette were the last ones left. Elle couldn't stop looking at the transformed school. It was like a fairyland, just as she'd planned. But the sight of all the giant red hearts made her sad.

What would Valentine's Day be like without

Hunter? Was he really going to leave her alone on the biggest night of the year?

She checked her cell phone for the thousandth time that day. There were no messages. She tried not to let it get to her. She remembered the way the cheerleaders had rallied at the end of practice. There would be a happy Valentine's Day for everybody! She wouldn't let them down.

"Your hard work paid off," Laurette said. "The school is unrecognizable. You'd never know how much bullying, incompetence, and stupidity goes on in here."

"Everybody worked hard," Elle said. "I had a lot of help."

"What are you going to do tonight?" Laurette asked.

"I'm making chocolate pot de crème," Elle said, "and marinating mushrooms. They need to sit overnight."

Laurette looked uncomfortable. "You mean, for tomorrow? For your Valentine's Day dinner?"

Elle nodded. "What if Hunter comes over after all? I need to be prepared."

Laurette put her arm around Elle. "He'll come."

"I hope so," Elle said.

Chapter 24

"CAN I HAVE a kiss, Elle?"

Sidney Ugman, Elle's unpleasant next-door neighbor and admirer, stood beside her holding some kind of plant over her head. It was the afternoon of Valentine's Day. The school party had been a big success. People partied all day, and the teachers let all the students out of their last-period classes so they could gather in the front lobby and dance under the disco ball. The whole school was having a blast.

"What is that?" Elle asked Sidney, pointing to the plant dangling over her head. It smelled minty, but not minty enough to cover Sidney's habitual bologna aroma.

"It's mintsletoe," Sidney said.

"Mintsletoe?" Elle said. "Don't you mean, 'mistletoe'?"

"I couldn't find any of that," Sidney said, "so I'm using mint. Kiss?"

"First of all," Elle said, "it only works with mistletoe, not mint. And second of all, mistletoe only works at Christmas, not on Valentine's Day."

Sidney's face fell. "Does that mean no kiss?"

"Sorry," Elle said.

"Try Chessie," Laurette suggested. "It might work on her."

Sidney shrugged and chased after Chessie, who was in line for some love potion. When she finally got a cup, she dodged Sidney and carried it across the room toward the spot where Chris Rodriguez, Homecoming King and school heartthrob, stood surrounded by girls.

"We'll see if this so-called love potion works," Chessie said to Elle as she passed by.

Chessie walked up to Chris, looked him right in the eye, and took a sip of love potion. Then she waited. Nothing happened.

"Did it work?" Elle asked.

"Tough call," Laurette said.

Chessie dumped her punch down the water

fountain drain, crumpled her paper cup, and threw it away. She walked back toward Elle and Laurette with a sour look on her face.

"It tastes terrible," she said. "I'm sorry, Elle. I should be nicer to you today. Nicer than usual, I mean. It must be so hard for you, breaking up with a guy like Hunter right before Valentine's Day, and then spending the day itself dateless, like a giant loser."

Elle ate a candy heart that said, BEE MY HONEY. "Actually, I'm having fun."

"That's right," Chessie said. "Let a smile be your umbrella. After all, you're our leader. You've got to be strong. And this whole Valentine's circus was your idea, after all. You kind of asked for it, know what I mean? Still, I can't help but feel for you. Celebrating V-Day in the face of so much heartbreak. You're a brave girl. I really admire you."

"Thanks," Elle said.

"I mean it," Chessie said. "I'm going to try the love potion on Chris one more time. Maybe if *he* drinks it while looking at *me* . . ." She trotted away.

"Still no word from Hunter?" Laurette asked.

Elle shook her head.

"Maybe he's planning a surprise," Laurette said, "a big, fancy, wonderful surprise."

"That would be nice," Elle said. But the more time that passed without even a text message from him, the more unlikely that seemed.

The dance music stopped suddenly, and Will Campbell took the DJ's microphone. "Hey, everybody, Happy Valentine's Day!" he shouted, and the halls of Beverly Hills High filled with cheers. "I just want to give a special shout-out to the girl who's responsible for spreading so much love throughout the school: your funny valentine and mine, President Elle Woods!"

The students whooped and hollered their approval as Elle made her way through the crowd to Will. "Best Valentine's Day ever!" he said. "Thanks, Chief! We all love you!"

There was more whooping and hollering.

Elle felt her cheeks go red. She took the microphone. "Thank you all," she said. "You're the ones who made this a great day. Beverly Hills High is bursting with love and Valentine's Day spirit! I'm the luckiest girl in town—because I have two thousand valentines! Now, let's dance!"

Everyone cheered, the music started up again, and Elle was surrounded by friends and well-wishers who all seemed to want to dance with her. *This isn't so bad*, she thought, as she looked from face to smiling face. Hunter or no Hunter, it was still a party.

Chris Rodriguez grabbed her hands and took her for a spin. Then Will cut in and twirled her around. She passed from partner to partner, dancing with everyone she could. Someone tall took her hands from behind and spun her around. And she found herself face to face with Hunter.

She stopped dancing. He stopped dancing. Together they stood perfectly still inside a hive of gyrating bodies, as if they were in a world of their own.

"Be my valentine?" Hunter asked.

Before she could answer, he led her off the dance floor and outside to the courtyard, where it was quiet. On the way out, Elle saw Chessie watching them, her jaw hanging open in surprise.

"What are you doing here?" Elle asked.

"I missed you," Hunter said. "I couldn't wait until tonight to see you. It seemed too far away."

"I missed you, too," Elle said.

"I should have called you sooner," Hunter said. "I was busy working on my sociology project."

"Oh," Elle said. "How's that going?"

"I'm off the project," he said. "Julia has a new partner. I'm going to find another topic to work on."

Elle tried not to let him see how happy she was to hear that. "That's too bad. Why?"

"Because the more I worked on it, the more I realized that Julia's idea was wrong, and by the end of the semester, she'll realize it, too."

"Wrong? In what way?"

"High school love can last," Hunter said. "That's obvious. All I had to do was look at my own parents to see that that was true. And at us."

Elle flushed happily.

"Any love can hit a road bump," Hunter said, "but it doesn't matter how young you are. You can make it last, as long as you make room for the occasional silly fight."

"Silly fight?" Elle said. "Like the one we had last weekend?"

Hunter nodded. "I shouldn't have gotten so angry, Elle. I know you wouldn't spy on me. Will you forgive me?"

She took his hands in hers. "Yes, of course I will."

"I'm so glad," he said. He kissed her. That was when she knew for sure that everything was okay again.

"So you're not going to the dance with Julia tonight?" she said.

"I never had any intention of going," Hunter said.

"You heard her ask me. But you didn't wait to hear my answer. Which was no. Even when I thought you might never speak to me again, I still said no. I like Julia, but she's no Buttercup."

They kissed again. She snuggled against him while he held her in his arms. "You're the girl for me, Elle. You always will be—my valentine."

Chapter 25

"THAT DINNER WAS delicious," Hunter said. He spooned up his last bite of chocolate pot de crème. "And this dessert is amazing. I can't believe you made it all yourself."

"Well—" Elle tried to decide whether or not she should admit how much Bernard had helped her—which was a lot. She decided that, in the spirit of romance, a little embellishment was okay.

Elle and Hunter sat side by side at a small table near the pool. The roses and honeysuckle over the arbor perfumed the air. Visible through the palm trees, a big full moon rose and reflected on the rippling blue water of the pool.

The night was warm and perfect. Romantic music

played softly. That afternoon, Eva and Zosia had helped her program her iPod with the perfect songs.

Elle wore a red velvet dress in honor of the occasion, with a black shawl wrapped around her to protect against the chill. Her Chihuahua charm dangled from her neck. It had turned out to be lucky after all.

Hunter looked handsome in a Prada suit and tie with a pink shirt. Elle appreciated the fact that he'd taken the trouble to dress up. It wasn't easy to get a college guy into a suit without a good reason—like a wedding, funeral, or job interview. Hunter had done it without even being asked. That was one thing she loved about him. He always knew the perfect thing to wear for every occasion.

Hunter poured more sparkling apple cider into her glass. "A toast," he said, "to the most beautiful girl in Beverly Hills. Make that, in the whole, wide world."

Elle clinked her glass against his.

Zosia appeared, carrying a tray, and cleared away their dishes.

"Sir? Mademoiselle? Can I get you anything else? More cider, perhaps?"

"That would be lovely, Zosia," Hunter said,

holding out his glass. "Thank you."

"Oh, and mademoiselle? You've got a little chocolate on your lip." Zosia dabbed at Elle's lip with a napkin.

"That's okay, Zosia," Elle said. "I can get it." She took the napkin from Zosia and whispered, "Remember, I'm not a little girl anymore!"

"Whoops. Sorry," Zosia whispered back. "To me, you'll aways be the little pink pussycat. And the chocolate is still there."

"I'll get it." Hunter took the napkin and gently dabbed at Elle's lip. "There. All gone."

Zosia disappeared, leaving behind a silver tray of chocolates and mints.

"You put together the perfect Valentine's Day, Elle," Hunter said. "I should have known you would."

"It wouldn't have been perfect without you," lle said.

"You know what?" Hunter said. "We just sur-ʳed our first big fight."

"Hey, that's right," Elle said. "We did."

"What doesn't break us up will only make us nger," Hunter said. "Now we know, if we ever ː a, er, disagreement again, that it isn't the end e world. We care about each other enough to calm down and work it through. Right?"

"Right," Elle said.

"I'm glad we agree." Hunter kissed her sweetly on the lips. "Mmmm. Still chocolaty."

Then he reached into his pocket. "And now it's time for a little Valentine's Day bling."

He gave Elle a small box wrapped in robin's-egg-blue paper.

Elle couldn't wait to open it. But first—

"I've got something for you, too," she said. "Underdog, come here!"

Underdog, who'd stayed in the house during dinner to keep out of the lovebirds' way, trotted out to the table with something in his mouth.

"He learned how to carry things without leaving teeth marks," Elle said. "For the movie." She took the package. "Thank you, Underdog. I'll see you later."

He went back inside, and Elle gave the package to Hunter. "I hope you'll like it."

Hunter opened his present first. It was a scrapbook Elle had made, beautifully designed, covering their history so far. It started with pictures of Hunter leading the BHH varsity basketball team and pictures of him holding the championship trophy surrounded by his teammates, cheerleaders, and Elle. Then there was a picture of Hunter and Elle at the prom, on their very first date.

"You were so beautiful that night," Hunter said, "but you look even more beautiful now."

Elle smiled and helped him turn the pages of the scrapbook. The next section showed images of their sunny beach summer: Hunter winning the surfing contest and Elle being crowned queen of bikini design; and Laurette playing guitar, winning the battle of the bands. There was a picture of Sassy, the baby seal Elle had rescued, posing with Underdog, and a picture of Hunter, Elle, Laurette, and Darren together around a bonfire.

"Last summer was the best ever," Hunter said.

"This summer will be even better," Elle said.

The scrapbook ended with a photo of President , victorious on election day, and Hunter in his UCLA basketball uniform.

osia will take a picture of us later, and we can at to the scrapbook," Elle said. There were blank pages left at the back for more pic- of more good times to come. Elle hoped she unter would fill them all.

ove it, Elle," Hunter said. "I'll always treasure k you. Now open your present."

unwrapped the tiny box and opened it.

She gasped. Inside was a gold ring in the shape of a heart, with a small red ruby in the center. It was the most beautiful ring Elle had ever seen. She looked at Hunter, her eyes shining. She couldn't speak.

"Try it on," he said. He took the ring and slipped it on her finger. It fit perfectly.

"It's gorgeous," she finally said. "I love it!"

She kissed him again. It had been a night of many kisses, with plenty more to come.

"You silly thing," Hunter said. "How could you think I'd fall for Julia?"

"Well, she's very smart, for one thing," Elle said. The ring sparkled on her finger in the moonlight. "And she seems nice enough. And she's pretty . . ."

"But she's not my type," Hunter said, "not m type at all."

"What's your type?" Elle asked.

"Petite," Hunter said, giving Elle a squeeze sweet. And plucky. And most of all, blonde.'

"Like me?"

"Exactly like you," Hunter said. "There kinds of love in the world, and they hav good points. But there's nothing like blonde

A slow song came on, and they dance moonlight. Elle had always loved Valentin

But this was the first time she had ever really appreciated what the holiday was about. It was the international holiday for people in love—and Elle and Hunter were more in love than ever.

Do Blondes Have More Fun?

Find out when you collect all the books in the Elle Woods series!